TIME TO
GO HOUSE

New York Classics
Frank Bergmann, Series Editor

TIME TO
GO HOUSE

by Walter D. Edmonds

Drawings by Joan Berg Victor

Syracuse University Press

First Edition 1994
94 95 96 97 98 99   6 5 4 3 2 1

This book is published with the assistance of a grant
from the John Ben Snow Foundation.

Publication of this book is by arrangement with Little, Brown Company.

The paper used in this publication meets the minimum requirements of
American National Standard for Information Sciences—Permanence of
Paper for Printed Library Materials, ANSI Z39.48-1984. ∞™

Library of Congress Cataloging-in-Publication Data
Edmonds, Walter Dumaux, 1903–
     Time to go house / Walter D. Edmonds : illustrated by Joan Berg
Victor. — 1st ed.
        p.   cm. — (New York classics)
     Summary: The adventures of Smalleata, the mouse, when she and her
family move into a house vacated by humans for the winter.
     ISBN 0-8156-0293-6
     [1. Mice—Fiction.]   I. Victor, Joan Berg, ill.   II. Title.   III. Series.
PZ7-E247T1   1994
[Fic]—dc20   94-17034

To Peggy Yntema
for her to share with Liza and Polly
if they love mice

Walter D. Edmonds is best known for *Drums Along the Mohawk*, but his many novels and stories about New York State have made him one of this region's greatest writers. Edmond's *Bert Breen's Barn* (Syracuse University Press) won the 1975 National Book Award for children's literature.

Preface

LATE one fall evening while my wife was away in England, I was watching our white Labrador from the front door of our old house in Boonville when a small sound warned me that I was not alone. I had turned off the hall light the better to watch Bridget; but there was more than enough moonlight to see two little mice playing the stair game, leaping wildly from tread to tread like tiny kangaroos. I had never seen anything like it before. They payed no attention to me but turned at the foot of the stairs and went scampering off along the hall towards the living room. I told my wife about it after she came home. She was entranced and immediately said that I should put it into a book for children.

Writers become used to people saying things like that, but I could see that K really meant it, and I began to think about the animals who shared with us the place my father had called Northlands, especially those who came into the house as soon as the nights began to turn cold. The year before there had been two half-grown mice who in late summer evenings liked to watch us from between the logs in the fireplace. When it became cold enough for us to want a fire, it was necessary each evening to pull the logs apart and literally shoo them out before putting a match to the kindling.

"I wonder," K used to say, "if they married."

And of course there were other creatures than just mice—like Reagan Ready, the fox, whom we had watched hunting the meadows for years. And the old bear I named Honeysuckle, who learned to open the door of the woodshed when there were apple peelings left over from the jelly making. I only saw him once or twice, but I often smelled him when he was nearby in the woods; a not particularly pleasant smell, either, something between sour dish towels and unwashed diapers. But he never did anybody any harm, though he seemed to have a great deal to complain about.

So I began to think about a story; and the next summer, when we were back at the farm, and my son's family were back, too, in their cottage across the brook, I started to write *Time to Go House*. On Friday afternoons, well before suppertime, my son's three little daughters, Eugénie, Janet, and Debbie, would come over the brook to listen to what I had written during the week. Another granddaughter, named Kate, who was staying with us in the old house, also joined in. And now and then, too, there were visitors. All the children wore their best dresses. They sat very still until I had finished, but then they wanted to see the places in the house I had been reading about. So we went down cellar to examine the hole between the foundation stones through which Uncle Stilton had led the mice into the house, and the room for preserves where the Rockendollar rats smashed all the preserve jars. Later we had to go into the attic to see where Smalleata met Raffles, and down again to look at the old and (I am glad to say) unused privy over the brook by which the raccoon had climbed into the house.

After which we would go back to the living room for tea or something colder like ginger ale or coke or raspberry vinegar, and the girls would want to know what was going to happen next. But even if I had an idea of that, I didn't tell them. No author, good or bad, would want to risk losing his audience!

So, all the animals were animals I had seen or, in many cases, known in or outside of the house—except for the unrolling of the toilet paper. That was something I had watched many years before in a cabin in the heart of the Adirondack Mountains; but I did not see why Raffles and Smalleata could not use the same method to get lining for their home in the Northlands house. Nothing in the story is fanciful. Only the way it is put together.

"So," you may ask or, if you don't, someone else will, "what about the Gogie?" You can choose not to believe he existed; that as a free American you have every right to do. But I firmly believe he is real, and I am just as free as you. He came through the window of my sister's bedroom one night of brilliant moonlight, top hat, green coat, walking stick, and all, and sat on the foot of her bed and told her stories. More than twenty years later he did the same thing in the same room, except that it was my son he visited. Peter told us at breakfast to explain what had made him so late. Peter had never heard about Aunt Molly's visit from Mr. Gogie, nor had I thought about it for over twenty years. But the circumstances nearly matched: the little man coming through the window in bright moonlight; sitting on the bed and telling stories, funny ones, Peter said, that kept him awake till daylight. The little man called himself Mr. Woogie; he had a tall hat and a coat with tails, though Peter did not say it was green, and he had a walking stick.

And then after another gap, this time of thirty years, granddaughter Kate was also visited in the same room and kept awake by a little man who told her stories. She was only five then. She did not mention the little man's clothes, only that he kept her awake for a long time.

So there it is; as far as the Gogie goes. As I said, you can believe he was real or not. I do. In another book I've told more about him and the fairies who lived in the brook which ran between the buildings and all night long made voices to lull your conscience as it rushed away over its granite slides and rapids.

Concord, Massachusetts   W.D.E.
April 1994

TIME TO
GO HOUSE

1

THE WOODS ended at the foot of the hill and from the edge Smalleata could look down across the meadow to the big white house with tall pine trees round it and farm buildings beyond. She had seen them there the first time she had looked out across the meadow, but before today it had never occurred to her to wonder about the house. It was just something that was there, like the pines and maples in the woods behind her, and on this still, warm October afternoon she probably would not have given it a thought if it had not been for the falling leaf.

It caught her eye long before it came to ground, falling out of the bright sunshine with now a sideslip, or a little twirl, but mostly just floating down towards the meadow, until it lighted on the grass only a few inches from her nose. Smalleata had seen leaves fall before, but this one was different.

"Why!" she exclaimed in high-pitched excitement. "It's red!"

"What do you expect? All leaves turn in October."

It was her Grand Uncle Stilton who took a nap every afternoon in the sunlight on the edge of the woods and it was Smalleata's job to keep a lookout for anybody that might come by. She did not mind doing this. Uncle Stilton was lying on his back with his hands behind his head and his round belly in its beautiful light gray waistcoat that looked sometimes almost white turned up to catch the full warmth of the sun.

Uncle Stilton was her favorite relative. Actually he was her Fifteen-times Great Uncle, but because he was such good company and because she loved him, she always called him her "Grand Uncle." He had the handsomest long whiskers of anyone she had ever seen and his tail, which was now curled through his crossed legs, made elegant flourishes when he walked.

Uncle Stilton was a mouse.

He was very old, and slightly portly; and Smalleata was sure that he knew everything there was to know.

"But what does it mean, when leaves turn red?" she asked.

"Some leaves turn yellow and some turn orange," said Uncle Stilton as if that ended the subject. He was irritated at having his afternoon nap interrupted, but he was also very fond of his young niece, whom he considered not only pretty and lively but sweet-natured. So he said more pleasantly, "What does it mean? Why, it means that it will soon be time to go house."

"What's that?" asked Smalleata, who had never heard the phrase before. "How do you go house?"

"You are full of questions," Uncle Stilton said grumpily. But after a minute he recalled that Smalleata was a very young mouse, three months old to be exact, and therefore could not be expected to know such things. Indeed, it was to her credit that she wanted to learn, and that being so, she had certainly come to the right person for information. He would tell her.

"All the better class of mouse go house in the winter," he began somewhat pompously, and then remembered that of course Smalleata had no idea of what he meant by *winter.* "Winter is when it gets very cold and the field gets covered by snow, and when that happens the human people in the big house go away. They go away every winter and leave the house empty. That," he said significantly, "is when we mice move in."

Smalleata gazed across the field at the white house and thought that it seemed very far away and she wondered how they would ever get to it. The field was a place where one had to venture with the utmost care once one got beyond the fringe of the woods where the holes and runways of the mice among the pine roots kept them safe from their enemies. It was an absolute rule that one had to stay perfectly still for several minutes before venturing into the grass: to listen; to look at the sky; to study the meadow; to make sure that there was nothing in the branches of the trees at the edge of the woods. An owl might be perched there at dusk, as motionless and gray as the dead end of a broken bough. When an owl hunted it was as hushed as death, except that sometimes the Great Horned Owl would scream wildly just before it swooped, a sound to freeze the blood of much bigger animals than mice. But at other times, especially when there was moonlight, the owls would hoot back and forth to each other for an hour at a time in a way that was almost laughable.

Though she had heard them often, Smalleata had never seen one; but she had seen foxes many times pouncing round in the deep grass of the meadow, especially the big dog fox who had his den on the far side of the hill. His name was Reagan Ready, and he had been near enough on one occasion for Smalleata to see his grinning teeth. "What is he pouncing that way for?" she had asked, and her mother had answered, "He is trying to pounce on a mouse." Just then Smalleata had heard a quick little squeak, and after a second Reagan Ready's head had appeared above the grass and he had gone trotting off with his long red tongue making libberly licks round his black muzzle. It hadn't been necessary to ask why he was doing *that*.

When she thought of having to go all that long way across the meadow, the sound of that little squeak and the sight of grinning teeth came back to her as if it were happening again right before her eyes. But it wasn't only foxes that made the meadow a dangerous place. There was the black cat gone wild that roamed in the woods and there were weasels. You had to watch out for larger snakes, too, and the black bear, old Honeysuckle, who came out of the woods on autumn nights and went mumbling and rumbling softly to himself down to the farm to try the smokehouse door when the farmer was curing hams and bacon. He had a great fondness for pork, but he was not above grabbing a mouse, especially if he found a nest of baby mice — mostly meadow mice who made their nests in the grass; they were slow and rather stupid and had short tails like a woodchuck. Uncle Stilton regarded them scornfully and called them gopherics, waving his own fine long tail to underline his point, for he and Smalleata belonged to the field mouse family and were therefore superior. Certainly, she thought, they were much better looking. But old Honeysuckle would make no distinctions. To him a mouse was a mouse.

The thought sent a shiver down Smalleata; for a moment her tail stiffened straight out. "Why," she cried, "everything in the world wants to kill us and eat us!"

"That is so," said Uncle Stilton. "Except human beings. They like to set traps for us and put out poison. They don't like to eat us as far as I know, so it's hard to see why they want to kill us. But then," he added, "men are the only animals in the world who make a habit of killing their own kind. They even have systems for doing it."

"But what is going to become of us," asked Smalleata, "if all the world wants to kill us?"

"Well, we have to be smarter than other things," Uncle Stilton replied. "And we are. Otherwise there wouldn't be any mice any more. We've had to learn to get along. We even do it with human beings and make them useful to us. That is the reason sensible mice go house in the winter." And Uncle Stilton took his tail in both hands and made an elegant arch of it over his head.

"Don't worry about it," he said from under his arch. "I shall know when it is time for us to go, and you will come with me. You and your sisters and mother and all the others I've taken house for so many years."

He looked so sure of himself that Smalleata felt there was nothing more for her to say. But she could not stop thinking about the journey they would have to make across the meadow, with Reagan Ready lurking in the darkness, or the wildcat on the prowl, or even bumbling old Honeysuckle making sad bear noises in the top of his nose. Whenever she came to the edge of the woods after that she would keep watch of the house. She would study the sky, too, for any change in the weather, especially to see if there was snow up there, whatever snow might be. She could not imagine how she was ever going to wait for the time to come, but at the same time she was afraid that it might come tomorrow.

2

THEN one morning she saw four human people in front of the house loading things into a car. There seemed to be an endless number of things to put in, but at last there weren't any more, and then two of the people got into the car with the old white Labrador dog who barked at the deer every morning, and the car drove away with the people in it and the two left behind waving and waving their arms at each other.

"They are going away for the winter," observed Uncle Stilton. "And now the caretaker humans will shut up the house."

"Will they do it today?" asked Smalleata.

"I expect so," Uncle Stilton replied. "That's what they usually do." But he didn't say anything about when it would be time to go house, and Smalleata was afraid to ask. Instead, she went off to play with her sisters and cousins.

They were frisking among the tall pine trees, playing tag over and under the laced roots, and at times they appeared to get quite wild chasing each other. Farther up the hill Smalleata's mother and some of the older mice were taking pine cones apart and collecting the seeds. It had grown quite dark in the woods. The sun had disappeared. Gray rolling clouds covered all the sky and way above in the tops of the trees they could hear a strong wind beginning to blow.

The air was getting very cold, and the young mice chased each other faster and faster. Smalleata felt her whiskers stiff and bristly and the littlest hairs in her soft gray coat seemed ready to crackle with sparks. When she had come up to join the play, she had thought the other young mice were being rather wild and silly, but now suddenly she felt as wild as they.

"Why do I feel like this?" she thought. "What is going to happen?"

Racing down the hill ahead of three other mice she saw something white and ghostly in the air ahead of her, floating just above the ground until it hit a tree root, where it rested white for a moment and then melted away. She had never seen anything like it before; but then she saw another a little off to one side, and still another above the second; and all at once the dark air between the pines was filled with the swirling, driving white things, and she stopped running to stare at them. As she did so, one lit on her forehead, just between her eyes. She could hardly feel it, only the coldness it left. "What is it?" she cried as she tried to brush it away.

"Snowflake," a gruff voice answered close behind her. Uncle Stilton had returned from his post at the edge of the meadow. He had a white powdering of flakes all over his back. "It has begun to snow," he announced. "Tomorrow night, if it keeps up, we shall have to go house." But he did not look especially pleased.

"Moving's a bother," he said.

Smalleata did not see why, but when she went into her family's nest she found her mother very busy and preoccupied trying to remember what she should do.

Once early in the night, Smalleata felt the urge to go outdoors and play, the way she often did on moonlit nights, when all the other young mice would come out, too. She stole away without disturbing anyone, but when she got to the door of their tunnel, the entrance was covered with snow and though it was absolutely dark, she sensed the snow still coming down hard. She even thought she could hear it, sifting through the pine branches with a soft *shishing* noise. She could tell it was not a night to play or dance in and after a minute she went back up the long passage and took the branch to the nest where her mother and sisters were sleeping, curled up in milkweed fluff and dry grass and bits of fern. Down another tunnel that forked into theirs she could hear the slow and pompous snoring of Uncle Stilton. Somehow it was a reassuring sound and instead of thinking that it would be sad to leave this lovely home, she crept in among the others and almost instantly fell asleep.

IN THE MORNING, it was still snowing a little. The world looked entirely different. The pine branches were sheathed in white and when Smalleata and the other young mice came out of their holes, they had to burrow up through the snow. It felt cold and was fluffy to walk on and Smalleata did not see how they would ever manage to work their way through it all the way to the house.

But the snow did not seem to trouble Uncle Stilton. When he saw how deep it was he just stood looking down at the meadow, holding his tail in a hoop over his head and saying, "Good! Good!"

"Are we going house today?" Smalleata asked him.

"Yes. Tonight."

Uncle Stilton then turned back into their place and Smalleata followed.

All her family, and especially her mother, seemed to be in a flurry of doing things. "Smalleata," she said. "You just must get your things together. And there are the pine seeds for you to carry." Everybody had something to carry, and down all the other passages she could hear the bustle of other people getting ready for the trip.

"Oh dear," said her mother, looking at her anxiously with one hand over the top of her nose. "I'm sure I have forgotten *something.*"

Smalleata did not know what to say, but fortunately just then she heard Uncle Stilton calling her and hurried up the passage to his nest. He was sitting on the grass edge of his bed which was stiffened with pine needles; he liked to talk about the hardness of his bed. He looked very much at ease.

"Did you call me?" Smalleata asked, glancing about the room which was all in confusion, with things lying about and even the curled beechleaf he used for a hat on hot summer days tossed carelessly into a corner.

"Yes, I called you. Nobody's paying any attention to me."

"But Uncle, aren't you going to pack your things to go house?"

"*I?* Pack? Why should I? I never packed in my life," said Uncle Stilton, scratching his ear in a rapid, offhand kind of way.

"But how did you manage to go house other times?" she asked.

"Well, there was always somebody who did it for me," Uncle Stilton said. "Generally your mother, I believe."

All at once Smalleata knew what her mother had forgotten. Her heart began to beat quite fast and she had to draw in her breath slowly two or three times before she felt bold enough to ask: "Do you think I could do it for you, Uncle Stilton?"

"I don't know why not," the old mouse said.

"What shall I pack then?"

"Whatever I ought to take."

"But what do you want with you?" she asked.

"How do I know what I shall want, or need?" he exclaimed in a testy voice. "Just put it all together and then put it into my pack-sack."

His pack-sack was made from a small pitcher plant, with a large acorn cap over the bottom to protect it when it was put down and a strap made of split and twisted timothy leaves to go over his shoulder. It did not look very large amidst all the litter in the room, and Smalleata thought, "I must choose just the right things, or there won't be room enough."

She tried to imagine herself as a distinguished old mouse who would want this or that at any given moment, but really it seemed to her that Uncle Stilton had the simplest sort of wants. He liked to talk and deliver himself of solemn pronouncements, but at heart he was modest, affectionate, and rather plain, so she began sorting through his belongings thinking of what she herself would like to take; and before long she had assembled some chokecherry pits and field peas and quite a small supply of oat grains, together with a few other objects that seemed interesting. These she packed in his pack-sack, and then lifted it to see whether it came to too great a weight. It seemed heavy to her, but she realized that Uncle Stilton was a male mouse, older and considerably more sturdy than she. She thought what she had done would be all right, and suddenly she felt as though she was on the threshold of growing up.

On top of the pack-sack she placed his beechleaf hat, though she had no great hopes of his wearing it; and then she went back to her own family's place and finished doing the things that had to be done.

4

It BECAME DARK long before Uncle Stilton gave the word that it was time to set out. There was no moon. Only a few stars shone faintly. At the entrance to their burrow the figure of Uncle Stilton was a dark and indefinite shadow, but even so she could make out that he was wearing his beechleaf hat. It pleased her very much that he should have adopted her suggestion.

Though she could not see them, she knew that mice were standing in the mouths of all the other burrows, waiting for Uncle Stilton to give them the word to march. Up and back behind the hill the sudden quick, high bark of Reagan Ready announced that he was out on a night of hunting. Uncle Stilton stiffened at the sound. Then he said in a high clear voice, "All right. Here we go." It was said in an almost casual way, as if he had not heard the barking fox at all. Only a mouse of great courage, she thought, could have spoken in that way with danger already approaching, and as she followed his sturdy figure down towards the deep grass of the meadow, she thought, "He *is* a great mouse"; and she felt proud to be his niece.

Snow covered all the grass of the meadow like a dim white damp blanket, and she wondered how in the world little people like mice could ever hope to get across it all the way to the house. But as he came to the edge of the meadow, Uncle Stilton simply stooped low and disappeared under the grass. Suddenly the snow was like a roof over their heads resting on top of the trefoil. In the underneath double darkness the stems were almost impossible to see, as was Uncle Stilton himself.

"Take hold of my tail," he told her, "and have the next person take hold of yours."

As she groped for his tail and found it in the dark, she felt someone behind her fumbling after hers, so she held it out straight till a hand that she thought felt like her mother's took hold; and then she heard Uncle Stilton's order being repeated back and back under the grass in soft receding whispers, until all the mice going house were linked together — so many of them she could hardly imagine how long the line might be.

This time Uncle Stilton did not give the order to start walking. He just stepped out, and it took a moment as each felt the tug of the tail in his hand before all of them could get in motion. But then at last they were on their way, winding one behind the other in and out of stems of trefoil and the tufted clumps of broom grass. It was perfectly still underneath the canopy of snow; on the damp ground their feet made no sound at all. Smalleata realized that it would be almost impossible for anything else to discover that their procession was crossing the meadow towards the house. Uncle Stilton had known just the moment to choose for making their journey, and her admiration for the old mouse grew even greater at the sureness with which he found their way. Now and then, when they were well out in the meadow, where the snow seemed to lie thinner on the grass above, occasional openings in the canopy let through enough starlight to show her dimly his stout figure trudging sturdily in front of her, his pack-sack on his back and his beechleaf hat cocked a little to one side. He made her feel such confidence that even when he stopped short and whispered to be still she was not particularly frightened.

"Shhh, shhh, shhh." The mouse voices were very small as they passed the word back along the line, and in a moment all of them were motionless. Then, with a chill along her back, Smalleata heard what had made Uncle Stilton halt his march — the shuffling thump of heavy feet coming towards them across the meadow, neither fast nor slow. Then she heard a plaintive sort of high-nose moaning voice saying, "Oh, if I could only find another bucket of strainings from apple jelly, I would be so happy. But I know I shan't. I know I shan't."

Smalleata did not have to be told who it was. Old Honeysuckle was on his way over the meadow to the shed where the trash and garbage barrels of the farm were kept. Eventually they would be taken to the dump back in the woods — a place old Honeysuckle considered it a personal duty to police — but, of course, apple-jelly strainings thrown out loose over papers and empty bottles did not offer as fine mouthfuls as they did if you could find them by themselves in a bucket. To find them that way was the next best thing to finding a honey-tree, and this late in the year a bear almost never found a honey-tree anyway.

The mumbling and stumbling came steadily nearer. She could hear the squelching sound through the thuds as his feet under his great weight crushed the snow into the wet ground. And then just ahead of Uncle Stilton, missing him by not more than an inch, she saw a great black hairy foot with long and dirty brown toenails stomp down through the trefoil and hit the ground with a spattering out of water. Just beyond it and a little ahead the other front foot came down the same way, and then the hind feet followed. The air was filled with Honeysuckle's smell, strong and rancid. If she had been a human instead of a mouse, Smalleata would have thought of old wet diapers, though the bear smell was much stronger. It stayed after he had gone, even after the last sound of his voice complaining about the absence of apple-jelly strainings had died away.

Uncle Stilton let out his breath.

"Close, but no cigar," he muttered.

And he gave the word again to march.

5

THEY were under the deep canopy of snow again where the only person who might possibly stumble on them would be Reagan Ready. But that did not seem very likely. Their trail was under cover all the way, except for the light snow in the middle of the meadow where they had met old Honeysuckle. There, of course, his tracks had made an open trench through the snow, but the smell of him lingered so rank that it was unlikely that even a fox could pick up their scent.

For more than an hour Uncle Stilton led them steadily on in almost ghostly silence. At the start of the trip it had not seemed possible to Smalleata that they would ever get all the way across the meadow. But now she realized that they must be coming near the far side, and she was not really surprised when Uncle Stilton stopped again, bent forward to part the grass, listened a moment, and then stepped forward into the open.

She followed to find that they were standing on the open road in front of the house, where the people had loaded the automobile with parcels. Between the road and the house was a wide, open space where the grass was so short that not even a mouse could have hidden in it. In fact it did not show at all beneath the snow. She felt it was a very unsafe place to be. The pine trees did not offer any protection at all. They stood too far apart, and there wasn't a single mouse run or burrow among the roots.

"We must hurry," said Uncle Stilton. "Tell everyone."

As the mice came out of the meadow, they gathered round Uncle Stilton and Smalleata; but there were still many in the line reaching back into the grass, and along it one could hear the whispered voices: "Hurry! Hurry! Hurry! Hurry!" More and more came running across the road to stand on the bare open space that Uncle Stilton said was called *lawn.* Only the tail end of the line was still in the long grass. But Smalleata suddenly heard something that made her shiver. It was like a sharp dry cough far out in the meadow.

"What is that?" she cried.

"What is what?" Uncle Stilton asked impatiently.

[18]

"It was like a cough."

"It must be the fox," he said. The last mice were just coming out on the road. "Run for the house," shouted Uncle Stilton. "Run for the end there."

At the end of the house was a screened porch, which came right down to the ground with an apron of lattice. The mice made a dark shadow on the snow as they ran across the lawn towards it. Smalleata did not see how they could get underneath, but Uncle Stilton cried again, "Hurry!" and she ran as hard as she could. He had taken off his beechleaf hat, and the pack-sack bounced on his back. It seemed a terribly long way off, and now they could hear something galloping over the meadow behind them.

As they came to the edge of the porch, Smalleata saw the square holes in the latticework. She jumped through one behind Uncle Stilton, who had a bit of a scramble, because of his pack-sack. But he tumbled through at last and the other mice came through the holes wherever they found them.

Looking out, Smalleata saw a long slinky shape streak towards her across the lawn. It was Reagan Ready. He came on right up against the lattice opposite her. He was so close that she could see the shine in his hot eyes and even make out his white and evil teeth. She hoped she would never be so near a fox again, though she knew she was now quite safe from him. They were all safe there under the porch. The problem was how to get into the house.

6

THE USUAL WAY used by the mice in other years was on across the lawn and down over a stone wall and under the big doors to the driveway that ran under the back of the house. Smalleata knew they could not be far from the big doors because her mother had described going house and how when you reached the doors you could hear nothing but the rushing water of a big brook that washed the back of the house. From the driveway there was a door into the cellar and years and years ago its bottom corner had been chewed out for a door hole. But that route into the house was impossible with Reagan Ready outside, and Uncle Stilton and two or three of the older mice huddled together to decide on the best thing to do.

It was utterly dark under the porch. Only the open squares of the lattice showed the dim whiteness of the snow beyond, and every now and then the slinking black silhouette of Reagan Ready, passing first in one direction and then returning as he kept up a patrol.

"We must think of a safe way into the house," Uncle Stilton began.

But immediately one of the mice interrupted him, not from the group of elder mice but from where the rest had crowded together against the foundation wall of the house, which had been built out of big, square blocks of limestone. It was a courteous voice, but also determined. "I think I have remembered a way we can get in. It is not absolutely safe, but I think we can make it nearly so."

"Who are you?" demanded Uncle Stilton. "Come forward, if you have anything to say."

A mouse came out of the gathering, passing close to Smalleata, but she could not quite see who he was.

"My name is Courtenay," he began; and Uncle Stilton said, almost impatiently, "Ah yes, Courtenay. Good people the Courtenays."

"Mr. Stilton," said Courtenay, "do you remember two years ago when several of us were with you in the cellar towards spring and suddenly halfway up the cellar wall a very large mole put his head through and swung his rubbly nose right and left and asked where he was?"

"Yes!" exclaimed Uncle Stilton. "I told him he had come house. He said his name was Wesley and pulled back out of sight. What about it?"

"This," said Courtenay. "The stones he came between were maybe an inch apart—anyway what was wide enough for that fat old mole ought to be wide enough for a mouse to get through."

"Of course," said Uncle Stilton. "But how do we find the hole?"

"I think I can figure that out," replied Courtenay. "Where he came through was about halfway up the wall, so maybe two stones deep below the ground. It was near the north corner of the cellar so it must be somewhere just outside the porch lattice. It has to be outside the porch because the earth here is just sand and no one could burrow in it. Therefore I think the hole ought to begin somewhere between the fern roots and the cellar wall. I'll go and look for it."

"That's dangerous, with Reagan Ready out there," said Uncle Stilton, and several of the old mice made little hissy squeaking noises to show they thought so too. Courtenay, however, was cool.

"If some of you go to the brook side of the porch, as if you were planning to make a run for the driveway, it ought to keep Reagan watching that side, while I do my scouting."

It worked out very well. Twenty mice or so started whispering and walking towards the far side of the porch and Reagan Ready stalked through the snow outside the lattice and then lay down at the corner, waiting for them to come out. Every now and then the mice would make a rush for the lattice as if they were going to risk the race over the wall, and Reagan would get slowly on his feet, his breath hissing softly over his licking tongue.

Meanwhile Courtenay had slipped under the lattice at the other side. He was gone perhaps ten minutes. When he came back Smalleata knew at once from his voice that he had succeeded.

"Everything's fine," he said. "I had to dig out the top for a little, but the rest of the way it's just as the mole made it, and it's quite easy to get between the stones. Now, sir," he said, turning to Uncle Stilton, "I suggest that two and three of us at a time go out and down the hole and into the cellar, and the rest of us will keep old Reagan interested in the far side."

"But what happens to the last mouse, with no one

to put up a screen for him?" asked Uncle Stilton. "The last mouse will have to take his chance," said Courtenay. "But I shall be the last." His voice was quiet, but very firm. Everyone accepted the fact that he would be the last. Uncle Stilton said only, "We thank you," and shook his hand. Then he called to Smalleata. "We'll go first, and remember no one talks when they have started for the hole."

Smalleata's mother came behind them. Uncle Stilton paused only to tell the rest, "Count your toes and tail three times over; then the next three of you follow. And so on. Good luck."

He wasted no more time. In a moment he had wriggled through the lattice with Smalleata behind him and then her mother. Outside the dark seemed stiff with cold, but they could see very faintly against the wall of the house where Courtenay had gone. His path led to near the corner of the cellar wall, where there were the mounded roots of a big clump of ferns. Between the ferns and wall, sure enough there was a hole. Uncle Stilton plunged into it. It went nearly straight down and his hat tumbled off ahead of him. But when it had gone down maybe eighteen inches, the hole leveled out and ran along the stones. Then it turned at right angles and Smalleata, following close behind her uncle, felt the big square blocks on each side.

Suddenly Uncle Stilton was no longer in front of her. But she heard his voice. "Careful, Smalleata. The wall ends and you will have to run down it, but only a little way. I am waiting here for you."

She felt for the edge of the stone, then scrambled

straight down. Uncle Stilton had her by the hand. They were standing on a pile of firewood.

"We are safe in the house," he said. "It will be easy for the rest, as long as Reagan Ready thinks we may go the usual way."

She felt a little shiver. Both of them were thinking of Courtenay.

Then her mother joined them and after her the rest in twos and threes until there were no other mice left to come. They had all been squeaking with excitement and pleasure at the way they had escaped. Now, suddenly, silence came over them, and Uncle Stilton called in a rather shaky voice, "Courtenay. Are you there?"

But no one answered.

They knew that in the end, Courtenay, who had saved them all, had been unable to hoodwink Reagan Ready by himself.

7

IN THE LONG SILENCE that followed Smalleata realized suddenly that it was much warmer in the cellar than it had been out of doors. The temperature was really delicious, and her first shock of horror began gradually to melt away. When Uncle Stilton called to them to come along, she was quite ready to follow him.

Uncle Stilton led the way down off the end of the woodpile. It was quite an easy descent, like going down a staircase of irregular steps. Just ahead was a huge gray enamel thing that went up halfway to the ceiling and out of its top came a series of round arms, if that was what they were, that stretched every direction through the cellar. Some seemed to go right through the far wall of the cellar, while others here and there turned up between the heavy ceiling joists and disappeared. It was the strangest-looking creature she had ever seen; she felt a little fearful of it; and when it suddenly coughed and started a soft roaring, she nearly jumped out of her skin. Even Uncle Stilton looked startled.

"This wasn't here last year," he said in rather an injured tone. "There used to be an old furnace over there, but it stayed cold. This must be something new."

"Automatic oil heat. We find it's a great convenience. Changes the climate of this cellar entirely."

The strange voice came towards them from a corner of the cellar. It was harsh, scratchy, and high. Then Smalleata saw a dingy gray shape approaching them.

At first she thought it was a mouse. But it was a great deal bigger than any mouse would dream of being. The shape was the same but the tail was bare of hair — not even a fuzz, and a sort of faded-roses color that seemed to her unattractive. Then, remembering things Uncle Stilton had said, she realized that it was a rat; and apparently Uncle Stilton was well acquainted with him.

"Ah, you're here I see, Rockendollar," he said. "I am very happy to see you." But Smalleata did not think he sounded especially happy.

"Yes, we're here. Moved in a week ago," said Rockendollar. He had long dirty yellow teeth that stuck out

from his mouth a good deal farther than one would have supposed convenient.

"Yes," he said. "Been here a week. Had to keep kind of quiet while the people from the other house were shutting things up upstairs; but it gave us a chance to see how this new furnace works. Doesn't have to be filled from the woodpile. Seems to run itself. Blows hot air. Man came down and took the end off one pipe which lets the hot air blow into here. But there doesn't any go upstairs any more." He put two fingernails up his nose at the same time and appeared to be in thought. "Furnace comes on by itself. Shuts off the same way. Don't understand why, but it keeps us comfortable down here. You'll find it the same way it used to be in your apartments, though." He gave a rather unpleasant laugh and his little eyes shone with malice.

"Well, glad to see you back. I expect you want to get settled."

"Yes," said Uncle Stilton. "We've had quite a journey."

He led the way round Rockendollar, who made no move to step aside, and all the other mice came behind him, walking in a circle round the rat. As she passed him Smalleata smelled a musty sour odor, as if Rockendollar liked to spend his time among decaying things. She was glad to get by.

From the cellar where the furnace roared softly away Uncle Stilton took them up a step and into another, darker one, one half of which had been partitioned off to make a separate room. From beyond the doorless entrance was coming a terrific clatter and commotion, mingled with uproarious harsh voices. The noise was enough to make anyone pause, but Uncle Stilton did not hesitate.

"It's the Rockendollar boys," he explained, "raising one of their rumpuses."

When Smalleata entered the room, she thought that Uncle Stilton had understated the situation. The floor was a shambles of broken glass, but on the shelves that lined the room still stood rows and rows of empty preserve jars. Peering out from behind them were the faces of six young rats. They looked a lot like the old rat in the furnace room, but they were leaner and not quite so scruffy. Their slit mouths stretched tight over their teeth, too, when they were not grinning; but they were all grinning at the moment and their eyes had the same wild and evil gleam, excited and violent.

Suddenly one of them let out a yell, squatting down behind the jar in front of him, with his shoulders to the wall, and then kicked out with his hind feet as hard as he could. The preserve jar flew out off the shelf in a long curve and smashed to bits on the floor, while all the Rockendollar boys yelled together. Then the next one had a turn, and again they all yelled and looked to see which jar had gone the farthest. To rats like them, smashing things, or any other kind of vandalism, was better fun than scaring kittens, and when they saw that some of the mice were shrinking back against the far wall, their glee was redoubled. They yelled and shouted and pounded each other on the back and started kicking the jars off harder than ever, hoping to make them crash among the frightened mice.

Uncle Stilton, however, remained cool. Even with a

jar now and then splintering close beside him he went on his way unhurried, erect, and portly. He had seen that the young rats just did not have the strength to kick the jars clear across the cellar room; the worst that could happen to any mouse would be a scratch from shrapnel glass. He even taunted the young Rockendollars a little.

"You'll have to grow up a bit more, boys," he told them, "before you can expect to scare me. You just haven't got the wallop of your old man."

"That's true enough," said old Rockendollar's scratchy voice just beside them. He had come in and now marched along, rolling from side to side, with a glittering glassy eye cocked at the shelves. "Lay off it, boys. Always scattering and ranting and raising hell," he observed. "Those dumb young snap-tailed bandits won't ever amount to a jig in Stittville if they go on this way."

Something in his evil walk and harsh stare daunted the Rockendollar boys. They stopped their shouting and let the mice go by without further trouble to the far corner of the cellar.

"Taking the regular route up?" asked old Rockendollar.

"Yes, it's the easiest when you have hand baggage," replied Uncle Stilton.

"Well, good luck. I may come up and see you sometime," said Mr. Rockendollar. "And I'll send up one of the boys with word if anything happens down here that might turn ugly."

"Thank you," said Uncle Stilton, politely cool, and he began climbing the rough stone foundation wall.

8

AT THE TOP of it, the house sill occupied the outer two thirds of the wall, so there was a comfortable space on which the mice gathered while they caught their breath. They were now above the Rockendollar boys and felt perfectly safe from flying jars; but the young rats seemed subdued and just stood among the jars looking up at the mice with curious eyes.

"Well," said Uncle Stilton. "We mustn't waste time."

He led the way along the top of the wall till he came to a hole in the board just above the sill.

"This was chewed out long ago by one of our ancestors," he explained for Smalleata's benefit and that of any other young mice who wanted to listen. "But some time afterwards, a family of red squirrels decided to try going house for the winter, too, and they enlarged this hole and all the ones above it going up to the attic— that's the floor at the top of the house. We are now about to pass the first floor," he went on, pulling himself up and into the hole, which was large enough to let his pack-sack through without dislodging it. "The second floor comes next, and then there is the attic."

The hole was like a round doorway. Inside Smalleata found herself in something like a shaft, perhaps eighteen inches long by six inches wide and going straight up. At each end the studding piece stood on end and would have made hard climbing with the wood grain running up and down. The outside wall was boards set tight together; but the inside wall was made of slats or lath about a quarter inch apart and between these cracks knobs of plaster came through everywhere. Nothing could be easier to climb and looking round the floor of the little space about her, Smalleata could see that this was the way mice had come for years and years. In fact there was a comfortable mouse smell there, and already she began to feel at home.

For an old mouse Uncle Stilton was surprisingly agile. Pack-sack and all, he was hardly out of breath when he came to the top of the shaft and hauled himself through another hole. Smalleata was right behind him and as she put up her hands for a hold to haul herself through, she glanced back at the long line of mice coming up the wall behind each other, each choosing the handholds that suited him best.

"Go on, Smalleata," said her mother. "You're blocking the way."

Smalleata went up through the hole; and now she was in a long, low passage formed by the ceiling of the floor below and the floor of that above, with the ceiling joists or floor timbers, whichever you wanted to call them, framing the space. They were about two feet apart and eight inches high. It was like a long, narrow ballroom for mice to dance in and as far as she could see there was nothing at all in it except Uncle Stilton, herself, and now her mother and the mice coming up after them.

Uncle Stilton pointed overhead. "There is the hole that goes up to the attic," he said. "You'll see that some other time. But now we had better get settled."

Several feet along the passage there was a mouse-sized hole to the left. It was the only one, as far as Smalleata could see, and Uncle Stilton entered it. Following on his heels, Smalleata found that they were in an almost identical passage between the floor joists. From it they passed on through yet another and another. Smalleata began to lose count of them and had a dizzy feeling of no longer knowing exactly where she was. But all these passages had nests of paper in them, mostly strips of newspaper, though some of them were brown, and the one Uncle Stilton finally stopped in front of had an outside covering of elegant, shredded, crimson wallpaper.

This was his own, and he surveyed it now with pride. The paper he had found in a roll on a cupboard shelf in the attic after he had nibbled his way through the board wall from the back, and he had kept his find to himself till he had completed covering his nest.

"You and your family are farther down the street," he told Smalleata. "I think I shall turn in now. I am a little tired," he confessed. "But we shall see each other tomorrow."

Smalleata said good night to him and followed her mother along the "street." Ahead she could see several other mouse houses, some on one side and some on the other, and a particularly large one near the far end which proved to be theirs. She thought it was very fine and even her mother modestly admitted that it was really quite commodious.

The entrance was at one side. Some of the paper shreds hung down from the ceiling and needed shaping back in place. In the family room was a large bed of cotton wool and bits of flannelette. It was a fine and cozy place and when Smalleata's sisters joined them and they were all snug together, she thought what a lovely place it was going to be to spend the winter. The Rockendollar boys and their old rat father seemed very far below. It was as if the trip across the meadow under the snow had happened years ago. It was hard to be scared even by the thought of Reagan Ready. Her mind began to swim. She was more tired than she would have guessed, and suddenly she floated off to sleep.

9

WAKING UP in a new place is a confusing experience for anyone, but it is especially so for a mouse. Field mice for the most part never go much farther from their home burrows than fifty yards, and the journey to the big house had been more than twice that far. The ancestor mouse who had first realized the possibilities of going house, and had led the first company of his fellow mice to it, had been not only brave but in the truest sense a pioneer. And the house itself was a wonderful place. Within its walls Smalleata would discover that she could make excursions many times longer than she had dreamed of attempting during the long summer days and nights when she still lived at the foot of the pine hill.

Now, as she opened her eyes, she could not think for a few minutes where she was. But gradually, over the faint stirring sounds of other members of her family waking too, things began to become clear. She knew that she was in house, and she also knew it was morning. Mice, who spend so much of their life underground, don't need to see light or the sun to tell whether it is night or day. In this as in other ways they are much advanced over many other animals, including human people. Smalleata knew it was morning and she wanted to get out to explore the new and wonderful place in which she was living.

But as happens in many families, her mother said that there were things she would have to do first. "We must get our home in order," she told Smalleata and her sisters, "and tomorrow we shall have to start bringing in more food. There are highbush cranberries round the house and chokecherry bushes down along the brook, and we must get the seeds and pits to store. Such a bother with so much snow to dig underneath."

Smalleata joined the family in chores because young mice are never allowed to disobey, but secretly she thought it all a hideous waste of time. As soon as her mother said that they had done everything that had to be done for that day, she went straight off on her exploration without waiting to find out if any of her family wanted to come along. She was not even aware of Uncle Stilton till she heard his smooth, throaty voice asking where she was off to. When she told him she was just going to wander over the house and find out where various passages led to, he said, "All right, Smalleata. But remember that you have to be careful here just as much as you were about the meadow. Always remember two things. Use the mouse holes whenever you can. There's not much comes into the house that's small enough to use them too. And before you come out of any hole, have a careful look all round for danger. Above you as much as anywhere else. Once in a while the farm people bring in the cat just hoping he'll catch some of us. He's fat and sleepy-looking, but he's very quick. And he has a way of settling down in a chair or on a table, just to watch the very hole you may be coming out of."

Smalleata tried not to sound impatient as she said she would be careful. But Uncle Stilton was not yet through.

"Another thing. Promise not to go below this floor today. You haven't been taught about traps. The people don't set them upstairs, only on the ground floor. But traps have brought tragedy enough to our family, and I don't want any more."

Smalleata then remembered something someone had once said about her father being killed in a trap.

"You mean my father, Uncle Stilton?"

"Yes, I do."

She felt suddenly sober.

"I wasn't planning to go down," she said. "I thought of going up to the attic."

"Go ahead then, but be careful."

As she went through the hole into the next space, it occurred to Smalleata that she had not really promised to stay above the second floor. But it was true that she had not thought of going down, either.

10

SMALLEATA found her way back to the empty alley that was opposite the shaft they had climbed from the cellar. When she came to the shaft itself, she saw that the squirrel-way led up through a slanting hole round the edge of a beam and once she was through that there was the same sort of shaft leading upwards. It had the same kind of inside wall made of spaced lath and knobs of plaster; without anything to carry she found it even easier to climb. At the top another squirrel-sized hole led through a thin board into bright daylight, and she eagerly scrambled through. She was in the attic.

It was huge. Overhead the roof slanted down on each side with hundreds of broad rafters. It reached the entire length of the front of the house and even from where she was she could see that there must be still more to it, opening at right angles towards the rear of the house where, far below, the rushing brook washed against the foundation wall.

"What a wonderful place for us to play!" she exclaimed.

"It is, at that," replied a voice.

Smalleata froze in her skin. She realized that she had completely forgotten all that Uncle Stilton had said. She had not looked round her before coming out of the hole; still less had she looked above. She was on the open floor, in bright sunlight, too paralyzed even to dive back

down the squirrel hole. The voice had come from somewhere overhead.

But nothing happened, and finally she looked up.

A young mouse was sitting on the corner of a cupboard that had been built down one side of the attic —

the same cupboard in which Uncle Stilton had found his crimson wallpaper, though naturally Smalleata did not know that.

"Who are you?" asked the mouse. "Where do you come from?"

"I'm Smalleata," she replied. "I've never been house before."

"My name is Raffles," said the mouse. "And I live here all the time."

Smalleata now saw that he was not a field mouse. He did not have the pale gray front that she and her family all had but was the same brownish gray all over. But she thought he looked nice just the same.

"I didn't see you at all," she confessed. "And Uncle Stilton had just told me to be careful before I came out of a hole."

"Well, if I'd been old Lennox, the cat, you'd have been in trouble all right," said Raffles. "But I'm not. And the house is shut up for the winter. And old Lennox is outside. As a matter of fact you can see him now if you look out the window."

From the window Smalleata could see the brook flowing down through the meadow, with the barns on the far side, and the driveway which came round the house crossing the brook on a cement bridge. A stout, very shiny, black cat with white feet and a white chin was walking over it with slow and mincing steps. He looked pompous and proud and she thought he would be cruel to mice.

"He's an artful brute," said Raffles. He had slithered down the wall of the cupboard and stood beside her

watching Lennox. "He'll wait all day, and you'll think he's asleep with his eyes closed. And then all of a sudden he pounces. He pounced on my uncle that way once. He caught him, and then he played with him. He would let my uncle crawl away, just so far and then he would spring and grab him. He tossed my uncle in the air with his paw over and over. Sometimes he just let him fall, but other times he would catch him in his mouth. And does he have *teeth!* Each time he bit my uncle a little harder. But my uncle kept his wits, scared and hurting as he was."

"Do you mean he got away from Lennox?" Smalleata asked breathlessly.

"Even so, it was only because he was lucky enough to be caught up here that my uncle did get away. You see, he knew where there was a new hole in the floor which an electrician had made to run a wire down to a room underneath. It had turned out to be in the wrong place and the electrician had run the wire down farther on. So the hole was there, to one side, where the slope of the roof made shadows. Each time Lennox let my uncle go he went a little farther towards the hole and each time when Lennox came after him he pretended to get weaker and so he moved slower, and this led Lennox to let him get a little farther off each time. And then, when it looked right, my uncle just as Lennox got ready to pounce again flashed off to one side and down the hole. All Lennox could do was put his paw down the hole with his claws ready to clutch, but of course he could not reach my uncle. My uncle bit his paw as hard as he could and Lennox yelled and pulled it out. My uncle got away," said Raffles, "but he could not get the taste of Lennox's paw out of his mouth. It was so rank."

Smalleata listened spellbound with admiration. She could not imagine how anyone could keep so cool while in such fearful danger. And then at the end to turn and bite that murderous paw was the most wonderful thing she had ever heard of.

Watching Raffles while he told the story, she thought how clever he looked. If anyone else could ever prove himself as brave a mouse, it seemed to her that he might. It was marvelous to have met someone like him on her very first day in the house, and she wanted very much to be friends. So when he asked now if she would like to have him show her round some of the house, she said at once, "Oh, yes!"

11

NEVER had Smalleata dreamed that there could be such an extraordinary place as the house. First Raffles showed her all the attic—there was a window at the back which looked down on the roof of a lower wing, with the brook rushing past its foundation wall. Over the brook was the farmhouse. So from the two windows mice could survey nearly everything important that went on. But the attic was fascinating too in all the passageways it offered to the floors below. Except where Smalleata had come up through the squirrel hole, the floorboards ended at the inner walls and all the outer framework was open. A mouse could go down anywhere he chose.

There was another, larger chimney that came up right through the middle of the wing that led back towards the brook. It had a funny, bitter-musty smell which Raffles said was left by bats. Smalleata had seen the bats appear in the summer twilight over the meadow, replacing the swallows, swooping, circling, and spinning, like skaters of the air. But it had never occurred to her to wonder where they came from.

"They sleep all day, with their heads hanging down," Raffles told her. "They crowd up there against the bricks under the roofboards. You can't see them and they don't make a sound till sunset. Then they begin talking in their little yittery voices, and pretty soon you can hear their knuckle claws scraping as they come down the bricks and roofboards. Then they fly round and round in the attic, trying out their wings till it's time for them to squeeze outdoors."

Smalleata thought it would be rather frightening to be there when the bats were swooping all about a confined space like the attic, big though it was, and she asked a bit nervously how long it would be before they came out.

"Oh, they won't come out now. They've all gone down to Texas for the winter."

"Where is that?" asked Smalleata, who always liked to be told things.

"I don't know," Raffles admitted frankly. "From what the bats say, it's a long way off. They told me that lots of people go to Texas, but most of them are bats. But I like it better here, myself."

"So do I," said Smalleata.

"Come on, then," said Raffles.

They scurried down between the studs and found their way behind a baseboard and went along till they came to a tiny hole near where a partition joined the outside wall of the house. Through this Raffles squeezed, and Smalleata followed him.

He was standing in a beautiful room. At least it seemed

so to Smalleata. And nearby was a smooth brown and shiny tree. There were three others, she saw, also growing in the room, and they were so unusual and handsome that she remarked on them to Raffles.

"Those aren't trees," he said casually, "though they're made of wood, all right. They're the legs of a bed."

Smalleata felt frightfully ignorant and if she had not been a mouse she would surely have blushed. It hardly made her feel better to have Raffles explain that this was not at all like a mouse bed, it was only the human idea of a bed.

"Unless you'd seen one with people asleep in it, I don't see how anyone would know what it was meant for," he said, tactfully. And he went on to tell her how one night he had climbed up and sat on the pillow beside the head of a man sleeping on it, with his mouth open and his breath rushing in and out. "It roared like anything," Raffles said. "Would you like to climb up?"

It was not too much of a scramble to get up on the bed, and once she was there Smalleata was delighted to see how flat and white it was. It felt soft under her feet, too.

"Does only one human sleep in this big thing?" she asked.

"No. Generally, there is a woman, too," Raffles told her.

"Don't the children sleep here with them?"

"No," Raffles said. "They sleep in beds of their own at the other end of the house. I'll show you where, if you like."

"But I think that's dreadful!" Smalleata exclaimed. "When I have children, they are going to sleep right in the nest with me!"

"That's the way it should be," Raffles agreed. "But human people do very queer things."

He led Smalleata down off the bed. There were other pieces of furniture in the room — a dressing table and stool and some chairs — but these did not interest her. Her mind was too much taken up by the cruel way in which human children were sent away to sleep in loneliness. She simply could not understand how that could be.

12

BUT AS THEY PASSED from room to room, Small-eata's wonder over the size and elaborateness of the house made her forget about the children. The room next to the bedroom held high chests of drawers. Then there was a hall, with a bathroom off it (though of course she did not know what a bathroom was). The cold, white, shiny tub and lavatory and stool looked somehow sinister and she shivered when Raffles said that once you got inside one you could never climb out because they were so slippery. Foolish mice that did chance to get into them stayed there till they starved.

There was something on a wall, however, that interested her — she did not know why. It was a cylinder of white paper in a holder, with a sheet at the front hanging down. She could not imagine what it was, but she was now feeling less shy about asking Raffles questions.

"Oh," he said. "That's toilet paper. My mother once found some in a cupboard and she thought it made the most wonderful bed she had ever had."

"It looks lovely and soft," said Smalleata.

"It is," Raffles said. "When our friends and relations

saw it in our nest, they all went and helped themselves. But now the people keep it in big tins we can't get into."

"Oh dear," Smalleata exclaimed. But then and there a fixed determination came into her mind that she would have a toilet paper bed when she came to make her own nest, no matter how difficult it would be to get some.

All the same, she felt easier once she was back in the hall. She and Raffles scampered along it together and through a doorway, only to find themselves in another hall, even larger. Oh, the house was a splendid place! To one side a stairway went down to a hall below, and above these stairs another stairway led up to the ceiling and a closed trapdoor which Raffles said opened into the attic where they had been only a few minutes before.

Opposite the stairs a door opened into a second bathroom, and Smalleata noticed that this one, too, had a roll of toilet paper on the wall. But they did not go in. Instead, Raffles went racing down the hall, which turned at right angles (the way the attic had above) towards the back of the house. Doors opened off it into two more bedrooms of which Smalleata had only glimpses as she ran past, but she thought they looked as elegant as the first one.

Then they were suddenly through another door in still another hall, with more bedrooms opening off it as well as a third bathroom. These rooms were smaller and did not look so grand, and Smalleata did not have to be told that here was where the children slept in loneliness. Yet she thought that in a way these felt more friendly than the other bedrooms. They seemed almost cozy, if anything resembling a human bedroom could feel cozy to a mouse. "Have you ever come in here when the children were sleeping?" she asked Raffles.

"Once in a while," he said. "But you never can tell what children will do. Once they caught one of my cousins and kept him the whole summer in a pail in cotton wool. Oh, they fed him nicely, but he felt very confined and was glad to escape in the end.

"It's best in summer to let the human people have the house to themselves as much as possible," he went on. "So mostly we stay in our own apartments and let them have theirs."

"Where do you and your family live?"

"Perhaps we can visit them tomorrow," Raffles said, and he started back up the main hall. "Here is where your people live, right under the floor here."

Smalleata would never have guessed. It all seemed so strange, and she had entirely lost her sense of direction.

He led her back to the first bedroom and the hole in the corner of the baseboard. Once more they squeezed through. But then he went off by a different series of holes until they came out after a while at a vertical shaft that looked somehow familiar. It was the one by which she had climbed to the attic, and she knew exactly where she was. Only now there was no climbing to do, up or down. She was on the same floor as her own home. She could not have told how they had come here; it was wonderful the way Raffles could find his way all over the house.

"Oh, thank you," she said. "I've had a wonderful time."

She watched him start down a shaft towards the ground floor. All of a sudden he was gone.

13

Wᴴᴇɴ she got near home, she could see Uncle Stilton visiting with her mother outside their nest. She was still walking on air, and her excitement must have been plain, for Uncle Stilton said, "You look as pleased with yourself as a mouse in a wheel of cheese."

But her mother said in a distracted voice, "You've been gone an awfully long time."

"Is it long?" Smalleata asked. "I never thought. I've had such a wonderful time. I met a mouse. A boy mouse," she went on dreamily. "He took me everywhere. He showed me the attic and the bedrooms and halls on the floor under it. They are right over us here, as a matter of fact."

Her mother and Uncle Stilton exchanged glances, but she did not notice.

"His name is Raffles," she said. "I'm going to meet him again tomorrow."

Uncle Stilton's whiskers stiffened slightly.

"Indeed?" he said. "And where does this young mouse come from?"

"From here," Smalleata answered. "He lives in the house. It's his regular home."

"Oh, I see," Uncle Stilton said drily. "A house mouse."

His tone dampened Smalleata's spirits a little. But she rallied quickly.

"He knows ever so much about the house. He knows just how to get from one place to another. He knows about traps, too. He's going to show me all about them."

"Indeed," Uncle Stilton said again. "He sounds pretty young to be fooling around with traps."

He had intended to teach Smalleata about traps himself and he didn't like the idea of a young stranger butting in.

"Well, I hope he's nice," Smalleata's mother said. She sounded a little sad. "Wouldn't it be a good thing if you brought him to see us?"

"Oh, I want to," cried Smalleata. "I want him to meet you, and specially Uncle Stilton."

Uncle Stilton looked somewhat mollified.

"Maybe I can bring him tomorrow."

So they left it at that. Uncle Stilton said goodnight and started back for his own house, and Smalleata followed her mother into theirs.

She was quite ready for bed after such an exciting day.

14

SHE HAD FORGOTTEN all about her mother's saying that they would have to gather more food to lay in for the winter, and instead of climbing up to the attic to meet Raffles next day, she had to follow Uncle Stilton and her mother with the other field mice down to the cellar.

It was an expedition Uncle Stilton obviously enjoyed

organizing. He marshaled all of them in the passage that opened on the shaft to the cellar and divided them into companies: one to go to the front of the house to pick up the fruit that might have fallen from the highbush cranberry; another to forage along the side of the house; and a third, which he himself proposed to lead as it was by far the most ambitious project, to cross the brook and go down through the shrubbery on the far side where the chokecherries grew as well as a few more small cranberries. They might even, if all went well, and there was no sign of Lennox, go as far as the farm garden to hunt out various sorts of seeds left from the summer's growth.

In his most solemn tones, Uncle Stilton warned everyone to keep a careful lookout, not only for Lennox but also for people and even such unexpected creatures as Reagan Ready. In the winter, when the big house closed down, some forest animals began to feel surprisingly bold about approaching it, even in broad daylight.

Then he went down the shaft to the cellar.

In the room with the broken jars littering the floor there was no sign of the rats, but Uncle Stilton said that was not surprising. No rats act lively till the beginning of night. But when they got into the room where the furnace was, a faint chittering above made them look up. There on top of the foundation wall was old Mr. Rockendollar with a couple of his boys. They had nothing to say. They just chittered. Perhaps they were asleep.

Here the three companies parted. The two that were to work close to the house went up the woodpile and climbed one by one into the mole hole between the stones. Uncle Stilton with his pack-sack on his back led the way through the furnace room which was so long it had a second furnace at the far end, but that one was not burning. Ahead was the door with the hole in the lower corner Smalleata had heard about. They followed Uncle Stilton through it and found themselves in a driveway with a floor of tilted cement blocks. It was cold, and wind blew under the doors on the west end. But the mice went out under the doors on the east side of the house; and as they came out, Smalleata saw the farmhouse ahead, and beyond it the big red barn and out-buildings. Between them and the big house the brook came rushing down a long slide and at the bottom churned and foamed in a pool. Over the foot of the pool was what human people called a footbridge, and their way lay across it.

This was the most dangerous part of the expedition, for anyone looking out of the farmhouse windows and seeing thirty mice crossing it together was almost certainly going to do something about it and if Lennox caught them there, he could easily capture half a dozen of them. But Uncle Stilton said something about nothing risked being nothing gained and rushed across the bridge as hard as he could run. The rest all streamed after him. Nothing happened. They were out of sight at once in the bushes on the far side.

Now Smalleata saw why they had had to cross on the bridge. The water of the brook, foaming and hurtling past the back of the house, had covered all but the tops of a few stones, and these were much too far apart for a mouse to jump — unless he belonged to the Dancer family of deer mice. And even if he did, and slipped from the wet stone into the water, it would have snatched him away in a moment and drowned him. She had never seen anything like it, so savage and strong. It made her shudder.

But Uncle Stilton told her impatiently to come along, and once she began searching under the bushes she quite forgot about the water. It was a beautiful day. Most of the snow had melted. The sun was warm, even if the wind blew cold. Two of the mice stood on the verge of the shrubbery to keep watch, but nothing happened. First they picked up the cranberry fruit, then they made a fine harvest of chokecherries, and afterwards Uncle Stilton and some of the most active young mice ventured over the open ground to the garden patch and found kernels of corn here and there, and pumpkin, squash, and tomato seeds. These had been missed by birds because they had been pushed into the soil, but Uncle Stilton and the other mice were clever at nosing them out.

They started back to the big house late in the afternoon, their cheek pouches stuffed to bursting and their packsacks and bundles full. No one saw them cross the bridge, though it took longer this time with all they had to carry, and soon they were climbing the shaft and adding their seeds and cherrystones and fruit to the stores brought in by the other two companies. The heaps about their nests made a beautiful show.

Everyone smiled. It had been a great day's work. And Smalleata realized all at once that she had hardly thought of Raffles all day. But harvesting winter food is as important a part in a mouse's life as making friends.

15

WHEN she got to the attic next day, Smalleata stopped
before climbing through the last board to have a careful
look as she should have on her first visit, and she saw
framed in the hole the corner of the cupboard with Raffles grinning directly at her. Her heart danced as she
pulled herself through.

"I'm sorry I could not come yesterday. We all had
to go out after seeds and things for the winter," she
explained.

"I know. We heard you going down to the cellar and I
had a look out from over the laundry and saw all of you
running across the bridge. Rather dangerous, I should
think."

"The laundry?" asked Smalleata, who had never heard
the word.

"It's the room at the very back of the house. The human people use it to wash things in," Raffles explained.
"You can get in over the ceiling from where we live, and
there's a funny little building at the back. It has a window you can look out through, but it's just like a chimney
over the brook. It has a shelf with a round hole through
which you can look down into the water and sometimes
see fish swimming."

This, though of course Raffles had no idea of what it
was built for, was a privy that had been built on for

convenience in the very early days of the house.

"I'd love to see it," said Smalleata, "and look down at the swimming fish."

"Why don't we go down now, then?"

"Let's!" she cried, and she raced beside Raffles down the attic.

"We'll go down the stairs," he said, "and I'll show you how we do it."

The trapdoor did not fit quite tight. There was just room for them to squeeze under, though Smalleata wondered if someone the shape of Uncle Stilton could have managed it. There they were, on the top step of the stairs.

Left to herself, Smalleata would have scurried down over the carpet, a step at a time; but Raffles stood up on his hind feet, folded his forearms and stiffened his tail up and behind, and jumped. He did the first two or three jumps from one step to the next; then he jumped two at once, and at the very end, three!

"Come along!" he cried.

Smalleata stood up as he had and folded her forearms. She raised and stiffened her tail. She wanted to close her eyes before jumping, the stairs looked so steep. But she knew she had to watch her step. So, with her heart racing, she drew a deep breath, and jumped.

It was easy! It was almost like flying! She jumped the next, and the next, and the next, faster and faster. At the very end she gave a great effort and jumped two at once. She felt like a member of the Dancer deer mouse family, or a bird, she was not sure which. She had never done anything so exciting in her life. She wanted to do it again right away.

But Raffles said, "That was good, for a first try. Hurry up. The second flight down is longer and much more fun."

So they ran round the landing and went flying down the second flight to the ground floor, and again at the end Smalleata managed to jump two steps at once; but she was quite sure she would never be able to jump three, the way Raffles did.

They were now in a narrow hall with doors opening out to the front steps of the house, a second into a high-ceilinged parlor with a dining room beyond it, and a third into the living room, where Raffles said the human people sat most evenings. He took Smalleata into it for a quick look. It was a very large room with dark green wallpaper that gave it almost a woodsy look and suddenly made her homesick for the pine hill. But what caught her attention most was something that looked like a big box sitting on a tubular frame with wheels. The box had a glass in it like a window except that you could not see through it.

"What do they do with that?" she asked.

"Oh, that's a TV," Raffles said. "The human people turn it on and then there's light and you see what is happening to other human people somewhere. We mice can't work it, but we do watch it ourselves once each winter when Mr. Gogie comes and turns it on. He likes to listen to the President give his State of the Human Union Message to Congress. He says it's useful to know what the human people are up to."

"Mr. Gogie? Isn't he a human if he knows how to work the TV?" asked Smalleata.

"It's hard to tell just what he is," Raffles said. "He's shaped the way human people are, but he's only about a foot and a half high. And he wears queer clothes and a beard. He has a high hat, and a green coat with tails, and knee breeches with thick wool stockings, and he always carries a cane. And then, of course, there's the fact that he can speak with animals, all kinds of animals, as well as human people."

"He sounds nice," Smalleata said.

"He is nice. He doesn't think a great deal of human people, though he says there's now and then a child in the house he likes to visit with at night. But he says of them, live and let live. If they don't treat him wrong, he doesn't put the trouble on them."

"Oh, I'd love to see him when he comes to run the TV," exclaimed Smalleata.

A kind of caution came over Raffles.

"Well, you field mice have never joined us at the TV times, but maybe *you* would like to come this winter."

"I would like to," Smalleata said.

But it turned out, as we shall see in a while, that all the field mice were to come. And in addition to watching the State of the Human Union Message to Congress, there was further and more important occasion for their doing so.

16

THE LIVING ROOM, with the TV lifeless, held little to interest Smalleata. Sheets covered the bookshelves and a strong smell of mothballs clung to them.

"We used to get a good deal of useful paper out of books," Raffles explained. "The human people didn't like it. So they put these smelly mothballs everywhere now."

He led the way out of the room and into the dining room.

"This and the kitchen are the places our family like the best," he told her. "This is where the human people eat, and as soon as they are through we come in and clean the floor of crumbs — and the table, too, for that matter, if they forget to wipe it. And sometimes we dance on the table. It's a great place for dancing."

The table rested on two pedestals, each of which had three feet, so it would have been impossible to climb up on it except for the chairs. Raffles showed Smalleata how to climb up; it was quite easy; and in a moment they had swarmed up onto one of its arms from which it was only a short hop onto the tabletop.

What a beautiful place it was, the wood all dark and gleaming; it made you want to step out with sliding steps. Smalleata saw at once why Raffles's family liked it for dancing. There was something about its being so high above the floor — all alone in the middle of the room,

long and rectangular, smoothly cool under her feet—
that was very exciting. She glanced at Raffles. He was
looking at her. Without speaking they stood erect,
touched hands, and went off for a turn round the
tabletop.

She was in a dream and she felt as if she would like to
dance forever. But Raffles stopped when they came to
the end of the table again, and she opened her eyes to
see a picture on the wall. She realized also that Raffles
was watching her, as though he had wanted her to discover the picture for herself. There had been pictures in
the living room, but they had meant nothing to her—
they were just things on walls. But now . . .

She suddenly saw that the picture was of mice, mice
on a table just as she and Raffles were, but on the table
there were also a big blue ginger jar and a magnificent
wedge of cheese. Two of the mice were at the cheese or
picking crumbs from the table. A third was standing up-
right at the edge of the table, and a soft light, which
might be coming from a burning wood stove, shone
against his front.

It was a grayish brown, like the rest of him.

"Why, they're house mice!" she cried.

Raffles nodded.

"Some of our ancestors," he said. "It gives the room
sort of a homey feeling, don't you think?"

"Yes, it does." Smalleata was lost in admiration of the
picture. The mouse standing up at the edge of the table
had, she thought, a clever face, rather like Raffles's. When
she said this, he answered, "There is supposed to be a resemblance. I don't really see why."

But Smalleata thought in her own mind that *she* could, and she was sure, as she had been before, that as Raffles grew older he was going to develop into a great mouse, perhaps like Grand Uncle Stilton.

"I love this room, too," she said.

"Yes, it's nice; but let's go on into the kitchen."

They scrambled down the chair and went across the room to the sideboard, under which Raffles showed her a spot where the floor had sagged away from the baseboard, behind which the house mice had engineered a hole and a passage. It was a bit of a squeeze getting into it, but the space was adequate, and in a moment they were coming out on the other side of the wall, right under a white enamel cabinet.

They were under the pantry sink, and inside the cabinet the pipes writhed down and into the wall like snakes.

17

To SMALLEATA the pantry seemed a fascinating place. It had a wall of cupboards over which were shelves holding all sorts of glass and chinaware. She could not help thinking what an awful mess the Rockendollar boys might make of them if they should ever find their way into the room and she hoped, with a slight shudder, that they never would. It was all too beautiful to be spoiled in that way.

But if the pantry was a fascinating place, the kitchen

really entranced her. She had heard rustling behind the cupboard doors in the pantry which she had decided must be made by busy mice. Here there were more cupboards behind which she could hear more rustlings. And there was also a huge black stove, for burning coal or wood, and a smaller white electric stove across the way — Raffles warned her that this stove was not a place to explore, even though there were crumbs under the burner bowls. A young cousin of his who had refused advice had got caught in the wires and been electrocuted there two years ago.

Once again Smalleata shuddered at the thought of all the fearful things human people made and did, but Raffles seemed untroubled. You had to learn and keep on learning. If you knew as much about them as there was to know, there was no reason to be afraid of them. It wasn't hard to learn about them.

"They think they know all about everything themselves. They think we are stupid creatures, and of course," he said with a grin, "a good many of us are and *do* get caught in traps or eat the poisons they put out for us. Come along, now."

They went the length of the kitchen, past the black iron stove to where on a large kitchen table a small mouse was busily tearing a paper napkin into convenient shreds. She paid no attention as they climbed up to her, but when Raffles said, "I'd like you to meet my friend, Mother," she looked round and replied in an abstracted voice, "Oh, it's you, Raffles."

"This is Smalleata," Raffles said. "This is my mother, Smalleata."

It was very correct, Smalleata thought.

The little lady mouse hardly took time from her shredding the napkin to look up. "I'm very pleased," she said. "Quite a charming girl." She seemed very preoccupied. When they were out of earshot, Raffles explained that she was almost always that way and it did not mean anything. But before they left the table to continue their exploration, Smalleata had a chance to have a good look all round the kitchen.

It was truly a wonderful room. It had an infinite number of smells in it. Some delicate, some spicy, and some were, well, the only word Smalleata could think of was "terrific." Besides these intriguing smells there were many other things to interest a mouse. There were a great many shelves, some stacked with pots and pans and more china; others held ranks of glass bottles, each of which held a lingering fragrance of one or another spice, and bottles of oil and vinegars of various kinds; and shelves in themselves were a fascination for any mouse.

Best of all was the table she was on. It was not long and exciting and made for dancing like the one in the dining room. It was covered with tan linoleum. But it too had bottles and jars in a rank at the back, beyond which a large picture window looked out over the brook and the bridge and the farm buildings. It made one feel much nearer than the view from the attic; in fact it was almost like being outdoors; and when she suddenly saw Lennox walking across the lawn, followed by the caretaker, she shrank back. But neither of them looked towards the window; they went on their way back to the farmhouse.

She could have stayed there looking through the window happily all day. But Raffles urged her to come down and go on exploring the house. So she followed him down off the table, and ran after him into another room where there was another table that Raffles said made wonderful toast crumbs when the human people ate their breakfast on it, but now it was not worth their investigating. Off this room there was a storage pantry in which, besides the monstrous white enamel boxes of a refrigerator and a freezer, there were cupboards right up to the ceiling. From behind one of the doors came busy noises.

"That's probably my uncle," said Raffles. "He spends most of his time in there, because it's where the human people leave a great many of their provisions."

Smalleata was curious to see what the inside of a human storage cupboard was like. Raffles said nothing could be simpler than to go and see. So he led her behind the refrigerator where there was a hole in the floor for the drainage pipe of an old-fashioned icebox. They went under the floor to the beginning of the partition against which the cupboard was built, and after a short climb came to a mouse hole opening into the top shelf just under the ceiling where several antique objects like butter paddles, vinegar crocks, and ice cream dashers had been put away to gather dust. Down below, the mouse sounds continued busily.

There was no problem about getting from shelf to shelf and on the bottom one they found a mouse standing on the shoulder of a tall glass jar trying to lift its tin lid. He was able to pry it up a little way with his hands, but then it always slipped back with a slight clink as his hind feet lost their purchase on the glass and he had to let go. It was these tiny clinks that they had heard out in the pantry.

The old mouse was so absorbed in what he was trying

to do that he never saw them till Raffles called out, "Uncle!"

Then he looked round and down.

"Ah, yes," he said. "Raffles. I'm glad to see you. Come up here and give me a hand. You can get up the wall just over there and come across the jar tops."

"I'll come right up," Raffles said. "But I've brought my friend, Smalleata, to meet you. She's a field mouse and has come house for the winter. Smalleata, this is Uncle Wensleydale."

"Ah, yes," said Uncle Wensleydale, still looking down from the jar. "Indeed."

Smalleata had a feeling that he didn't really see her at all.

He was a thin mouse with a face slightly puckered with age and very bright small eyes. She thought he looked a bit like Raffles, but there was a stronger resemblance to the mouse in the picture in the dining room. And he sounded so vague that she wondered whether his terrible encounter with Lennox might not have affected his mind. Yet he looked kind, especially when he remarked with a slight quiver of his whiskers that field mice were fine people. Then he seemed to forget her entirely and called to Raffles to come and help him.

They climbed together up the wall and while Raffles joined his uncle on the jar Smalleata sat on the lid of the next one and looked on. In only a moment she decided there was nothing vague about Uncle Wensleydale at all. He was just too much absorbed in his problem to think of anything else.

Raffles took his place opposite Uncle Wensleydale and

both lifted the lid together. They nearly got it off, but then their feet slipped and the lid settled back with the familiar little clink, while the two mice barely saved themselves from sliding off the jar entirely.

Smalleata said suddenly, "Would it work better if you were on the same side, if I joined you for that matter, and we all lifted and shoved together? Then it would slide right off."

Uncle Wensleydale regarded her with his sharp little eyes.

"You've got an idea, I think," he said. "Let's try it. You're the strongest of us, Raffles, so you take the middle."

It worked. With three together, the lid lifted easily. They shoved, and when it came down, it was cocked halfway off the mouth of the jar. Another push and it slid off entirely and clattered down between the cupboard door and the shelf.

"That was clever of you," Uncle Wensleydale said approvingly. And he leaned over to look into the jar. The rolled grains of the oatmeal came almost to the top. Putting down his hands he brought up a double handful and passed some to both Smalleata and Raffles.

Smalleata had never tasted anything like it. She thought it delicious and said so.

"Nourishing," said the old mouse. "It keeps up the energy."

As if it had done just that he suggested that now they had learned the trick and were all there together it would be a good thing to take all the lids off all the jars, which they did, making a fine clatter.

Most of the jars were full of cornmeal, or rice, or spaghetti, or hominy, or dry cereal, or some other thing equally good for a mouse. Uncle Wensleydale said he could never remember a time when so much food had been available to bring them through the winter.

"And largely due to this young lady," he said, and Smalleata glowed with pride.

18

THEY DID NOT get to see the big trout below the privy that day, and by the time they finally came to look for him he had gone away — probably to one of the deep holes so as not to be caught in shallow water when the brook froze over.

While they were going back, disappointed, above the laundry ceiling, Smalleata became aware of a smell she had never met before, but which reminded her of something just the same. It was fairly strong; it had a kind of sour quality, like unwrung dishcloths, but it was also tangy, something that had been left there by some animal very much alive. She suddenly remembered the night they came to the house and old Honeysuckle, the bear, passed just above them and she knew that that was what she had been thinking of. This smelled a bit like bear, though not so rancid. It was a more comfortable sort of smell, almost mousey, but she could tell it did not come from a mouse for her skin was crimping along the back of her neck.

"Do you know what it is?" she asked Raffles. "I did not see it when it came in here, but Uncle Wensleydale said it was a raccoon smell."

"Oh," said Smalleata, who had never seen one.

"I've never seen one, either," Raffles said. But his uncle had told him that raccoons looked and walked something like bears. The difference was, besides their being much smaller, though a great many times the size of a mouse, that they had large ears, bushy black and white ringed tails, and their front feet were more like hands on people, or for that matter a little like the front feet of mice.

"They must be peculiar," Smalleata observed.

"I guess they must be. They eat everything, corn, fruit, fish, frogs, worms — and mice," Raffles added ominously. "But we won't have to worry about her here in the house, even if she does come to make her home here. She can't move fast, like a mouse, under the floors."

"You mean she might come house, too?" asked Smalleata.

"Well, that might be why she came exploring. Uncle Wensleydale said she might be looking for a place to hibernate in."

"Hibernate? Oh, you mean to winter-sleep the way old Honeysuckle does!"

"It's about time for them to start," Raffles said. "Usually raccoons use hollow branches in dead trees. They sleep there all winter, and in the spring they have their babies and only bring them down when they are ready to help hunt."

Smalleata's curiosity was powerfully aroused. Raccoons sounded such odd animals, both in their shape and their habits. A bushy, ringed tail! She would like to get a good look at one. And then their eating habits. She was not much distressed over their including mice in their diet when they could — no raccoon would ever catch her, ever, not here in the house.

She went on after Raffles over the laundry towards the kitchen pantry, and by the time they got back to Uncle Wensleydale, still fussing over his open jars of cereals and flour, she had almost forgotten the strange smell of the raccoon.

19

IN NOVEMBER the snow came in earnest. It fell without ceasing all day and all night. Sometimes it snowed for three days at a time, driving before the northwest wind while the pine trees about the house swayed their long branches and sighed from the strain. The snowflakes flew past the attic windows so hard and fast that to Raffles and Smalleata, sitting on the sills and looking out, it seemed as if the house itself were moving upwards in the opposite direction and flying through the sky.

When night came and it cleared, the meadows glistened in the moonlight and Smalleata and Raffles saw

old Honeysuckle knocking open the door of the woodshed
where the farmer's garbage cans were kept till taken to
the dump. After a moment Honeysuckle reappeared,
stumbling a little, for he was clutching a can to his chest
with his forearms. He did not notice the high sill that

had to be stepped over, so he tripped and fell flat on the can which burst open and covered his front with swill. He seemed dazed and just sat wiping his front with his paws and licking them clean.

The two little mice could imagine the whining complaints he must be making to himself, but of course at that distance and through the closed window, they could not hear him. Then suddenly floodlights came on from the farmhouse wall, showing him sitting there, a sagging black body on the white snow with a circle of swill in front of him and his muddled eyes blinking at the lights. It was so funny, Smalleata wanted to laugh, but just then there was a flash and a roar, followed by a second. The farmer was shooting his shotgun.

It did not hurt Honeysuckle, though the shot peppered his thick hide as hard as hail. He scrambled up and vamoosed, leaving a broad trail in the snow, partly of garbage, and mostly of indignation. They did not see him again. When she told Uncle Stilton about it, he said, "He'll probably not be back this year. A thing like that is enough to make anyone want to hibernate right away."

And probably he did so, for now the winter had closed upon the farm and gripped the house until at nights the rafters creaked in the roof and on some nights the small hard flakes of snow scrabbled over the shingles like the toenails of racing mice. Raffles and Smalleata played through the attics, especially on moonlit nights, when the air was so crisp and cold and brittle that their hair seemed to be standing on end. Some nights they went down the stairs and played the stair game, and often other young mice would join them, until there were perhaps fifteen or twenty flying down the stairs in a stream, with their tails out and their breaths making little ghosts of clouded air in front of them, almost like bits of cotton wool; and all of a sudden Smalleata realized that the time had come when she must introduce Raffles to her family.

20

RAFFLES came next morning by the vertical shaft beside the chimney, which was the principal route by which all mice and other animals moved up or down in the house, and Smalleata was waiting for him when he pulled himself up onto the lath and plaster which was the mouse's floor but the humans' ceiling. She felt suddenly shy. As she led Raffles through the various holes from one alley to another between the joists, she was aware of the other field mice all watching them. She seemed to hear them whispering, "Look at who Smalleata has with her." And she realized then how different Raffles looked from her relations. But all of a sudden she did not care. No matter what her mother and Uncle Stilton might be going to say, she felt gay and proud.

Uncle Stilton and her mother were sitting talking outside of his red paper nest; somehow she thought it looked particularly handsome today. She glanced at Raffles to see if he was impressed, but it was impossible to tell. He seemed much more self-possessed than she was.

The two older mice turned towards them as they approached.

"Mother, Uncle Stilton," she said, "this is Raffles."

Her mother gave him a blank stare.

"So you're the young person who's been taking so much of our little Smalleata's time!" she said, in a faraway voice.

"I'm afraid I am," Raffles replied cheerfully. "We've had a lot of fun."

"Indeed!" Smalleata's mother exclaimed. Her voice if anything was smaller than before.

Uncle Stilton cleared his throat.

His long tail came up and made a graceful curve behind his head. He looked remarkably elegant, even for him.

"How do you do?" he asked formally, looking Raffles straight in the eye. "You seem to have shown our little girl about quite a lot."

"Yes, I know," Raffles admitted. "But it seems like a good idea for her to learn all about the house if she's going to live here."

Smalleata marveled at how cool he kept under all this questioning — as cool, she thought, as Uncle Wensleydale must have been in the jaws and claws of Lennox — and all at once she realized how comforting it would be to have someone with such a cool head to look after her.

But her mother cried out in a small, shrill voice, "Oh, no! No!"

She was clasping her hands tight over her breast and her glance darted in agitation from one to another. Uncle Stilton was put out by her manner.

"*Now*, what's the matter?" he wanted to know.

"She won't go back across the meadow with us in the spring. She won't be in our nest any more on the hill. We'll never see her again." And her little voice trailed tremulously into silence. It made Smalleata feel quite sad for a moment.

"She'll live here." Smalleata's mother found her voice again, but so near a whisper it was hard to hear. "And she'll . . . Her children . . . They'll . . . They'll not be *field* mice!"

"I don't see the point of getting onto the children this early," said Uncle Stilton. "But they'll be Smalleata's when she has them, and that's half the battle."

When upset, Uncle Stilton was apt to get a little free with his figures of speech. "We don't," he went on, "need to drop the portcullis before the horse is stolen. Raffles seems to me to have the makings of a fine young mouse. How do *you* feel about it, Smalleata?"

"I have to be where my heart is, Uncle Stilton," she surprised herself by saying, "and Raffles has it now."

For the first time Raffles looked slightly embarrassed. But he said, "I feel the same way about her."

"Then why," asked Smalleata's mother, "can't *she* take *his?* Then they could come back to our hill and be field mice."

Uncle Stilton said, "No, Raffles is a house mouse. This is his home. He understands it. He knows how to look out for himself here, and consequently for his family, when he'll get them. I like what you said, Smalleata. If you're serious, this is where you ought to be."

The tip of Smalleata's mother's nose and her whiskers

quivered with rebellion. "But we don't know *anything* about this young mouse!" she exclaimed.

Raffles cleared his throat, though some people might have thought he had squeaked. "I was going to ask, if you think it proper, if I could bring my uncle here to meet you."

"A fine idea," said Uncle Stilton. "I should like to meet him very much. Meanwhile, there's no rush that I can see about having to make decisions," and he looked at Smalleata encouragingly and arched his tail elegantly over his back.

21

UNCLE WENSLEYDALE was not in his favorite haunt in the kitchen pantry cupboards, where he could gloat over the opened jars of cereals. When they finally ran him to ground, he was in a corner of the room in which the human people ate their breakfasts, but where, of course, now that they were gone, no toast crumbs were to be expected.

The old mouse was crouched in the middle of a register on the floor through which, in spite of the fact that the furnace flue was supposed to be shut off, a little warmth was sifting, and this morning for once the matter of food was not on his mind.

"Hello there, Raffles," he said as soon as he caught sight of them. "I was hoping you'd turn up. I think it's time to declare trap day. The man from over the brook hasn't been in for a week, and then he didn't trouble to look at the traps. I say it's time to spring them."

His eyes passed over Smalleata as if she weren't there, but Raffles added, after he had agreed about springing the traps, "I'd like Smalleata to come along too. So she can learn how traps work."

Uncle Wensleydale at that allowed himself to see her.

"Well, all right," he said, rather grudgingly, "as long as she keeps out of the way. Trap-springing is a job for men mice, and only a few understand it. My grandfather taught me, and I've taught you, Raffles, and it's not properly something for female mice to have a part in. But bring her along, if you want to."

Raffles made his mouth into a tight circle, which pointed his whiskers straight forward, but he didn't say anything; and Uncle Wensleydale suddenly twitched and whisked off the register. He was very brisk in all his motions.

Now he led them into a little back hall, at the end of which Smalleata could see that there was another very large room up two steps. Raffles said it was a study for the man of the house, who wrote letters and other things on a machine, day after day. But Uncle Wensleydale was not one to tarry for such explanations. He had whisked into a very small room with a basin and another water closet in it.

Beside the last there was a pipe stack for ventilation with an opening in the floor to let it past, and this had been so casually cut out that there was plenty of room for a small active mouse to squeeze down through. With a determined push of his hind legs the old mouse did so and the two younger ones followed.

They were now underneath the floor, heading back towards the breakfast room, but presently Uncle Wensleydale scrabbled up the side of a joist and disappeared through a hole in the floor above. Smalleata and Raffles climbed after him and found him seated on the floor of a closet. It was not at all a cupboard, but a real closet with a door that had a faint thread of light under it. Smalleata did not need to be told that it opened back into the breakfast room they had just left. It was wonderful how Raffles and Uncle Wensleydale were able to make use of closed rooms without being dependent upon doors.

This closet had a very special smell, too; or to be more accurate a delicious bouquet of smells. One scent seemed to be at the center of all the others, the body, so to speak, of the whole wonderful scent of the closet. Raffles said it was soap. She thought it divine, and when she told him, he said he would try to find some odd cakes in the bathrooms upstairs.

She had smelled those already, however, and the smell of used soap cakes on basins was not at all the same as this marvelous exhalation that came, she discovered at once, from a large new iron trash barrel in one corner. "It's a pity that the lid is something even you can't find out how to take off," said Uncle Wensleydale, and for the first time that morning there was a look of approval in his eyes.

Besides the soap smell, there were others just as fascinating. There was a high spice something that brought wrinkles in her nose and upper lip; Raffles said it was curry, a powder no mouse could eat; but coming from a closed tin she found it fascinating. There was a strange foreign odor, too, a little sour, a little fruity — it seemed in a peculiar way to bring sunlight to her mind — which came from the end of one of a long line of bottles lying on their sides. Uncle Wensleydale explained that it was wine seeping through a cork that was not exactly what it ought to be. "Nor would you be, either," he told her brusquely, "if some of that stuff got inside of you." But Smalleata thought she would like to try it sometime, just to see.

Then there were rows and rows of jellies, jams, marmalades, and pickles, all of different colors and shapes, and each with its own smell. She felt quite dizzy with so much deliciousness surrounding her, until Uncle Wensleydale's dry voice brought her to her senses.

"When one looks at all this," he commented, "one can understand why human people feel they have to put traps here. Come on, Raffles. We might as well get to work."

It took Smalleata a moment to realize that what she was looking at was a trap. It looked so innocent, like a low eight-sided house of pinkish wood, with a round door in every other side and a faint but pleasant smell of cheese. Uncle Wensleydale, however, approached it with every manifestation of disgust and contempt. When he had concluded this ceremony, Raffles took Smalleata to one of the doorways. "Look inside," he told her, "But don't *go* in." She did so.

Just beyond her reach and stuck on a wire that came down from the ceiling of the little house was a piece of cheese; in fact, as she looked closer, she saw that there were four nuggets of cheese, each on its wire and one for each door. She was entranced; it was such a neat and symmetrical arrangement.

"Lots and lots of mice like you have thought what a lovely little house," said Raffles's voice above her. He and Uncle Wensleydale had skipped on top of the little house and were leaning over an arrangement of stiff wires. Uncle Wensleydale reached out his front paw and touched one of the wires.

Instantly there was a frightening *SNAP*, as sharp and horrifying as a tiny snap of lightning, and Uncle Wensleydale was peering at her from under a cross wire, attached to others that had sprung up making a kind of bridge on top of the house. As he met her eyes a kind of conniving grin came over him; it seemed to show even in the stiff sweep up of his tail; Uncle Wensleydale was obviously enjoying his job.

"Now, Smalleata," Raffles said. "You look closely through the door, but don't put your head in. And watch."

He reached among the wires as Uncle Wensleydale had done, pushed, and the snap came instantly. But Smalleata's sharp eyes had seen the wire loop leap up against the ceiling.

"If you were after the cheese, your neck would be inside that loop," Raffles said. "And you would be strangling."

He needn't have added the last. Smalleata could see for herself, only too plainly. She shivered uncontrollably. By the time she was able to collect herself, Raffles and

Uncle Wensleydale had sprung the other two parts of the trap and were climbing to another shelf.

Here there was a trap of an entirely different shape. It had a flat wooden base about two inches by four, with a wire frame of copper on a powerful spring that crossed the middle of the base. The frame, in other words, covered half the base, whether it was drawn open or had closed. It was now open and held so by an arm of wire that crossed the middle crosspiece and was caught by an uplifted pan on the other side of the spring. On the pan was a piece of cheese, a bit dry by now, but still with an authentic, if faint, aroma.

"Well, Raffles," said Uncle Wensleydale. "How about your tackling this one?"

Grinning, Raffles said, "All right"; but Smalleata saw at once that he was deadly serious as he approached the trap.

"You see, Smalleata," Uncle Wensleydale explained, "you mustn't allow any part of you to get in reach of the big springing frame. If you come at it from the front or sides, it's got you. You're just gone, that's all."

Like many dangerous things, the handling of it was simple, once one had learned the necessity of extreme carefulness. Moving cautiously, one foot at a time so that the trap was not disturbed in the slightest way, Raffles stepped over the set frame until all four feet were inside and he was standing beside the tongue wire that held the spring set. At the same time, as a precaution, he brought his tail over his back and took the end of it in his mouth. Then with his left front foot he reached forward over the center spring and pushed down on the pan that held the cheese.

What happened next came too fast for Smalleata to follow. She saw the trap base lift from the shelf and the square wire frame flash over Raffles's back in a violent arc. It came down on the wooden base with a crack like the world splitting open. Her heart stopped for what seemed three whole beats. It was impossible that Raffles had not been hurt.

But he had not been. When she could bear to look again, he was stepping off the trap which now looked empty and harmless. He pulled the cheese off the pan and brought it over and divided it with her. It was dry and had a tendency to crumble in her hands but she thought it perfectly delicious.

Uncle Wensleydale watched them with his twinkling eyes.

"One of the advantages of being small, like a house mouse, is that you can get inside that spring," he said. "Well if you've, finished that cheese, there's lots more traps to spring."

They spent almost all the morning going from place to place where the human people had set traps. All were either the little house kind or the kind that Raffles had sprung. He and his uncle took turns springing those, and Smalleata could never bring herself to watch them. She kept her eyes closed till she heard the terrible snap and then opened them each time with the same trembling apprehension. The other traps seemed to her easy; she felt she could have sprung them herself; but the powerful single traps remained utterly terrifying and she resolved, if she ever had little mice of her own, never to let them even go near one.

Finally they came to what Uncle Wensleydale said was the last trap. It was on top of the bookcase in the living room, and when they had climbed up by the sheets that had been hung over the front to keep the books from dust, she saw that it was altogether a different sort of thing. It was made of nickel and was shaped like two oval jaws, each with jagged triangular teeth that obviously fitted into each other when the jaws were closed, and in the middle was a pan holding a bit of cheese and looking like the tongue in the mouth of a shark or some equally awful creature.

Uncle Wensleydale sat down and began scratching his ear with a hind leg. He admitted frankly that he had never seen a trap like it in all his life.

"I've been studying it three or four times, Raffles," he said. "There's no safe way to reach in and spring the pan. It's got me baffled."

Raffles studied it too. But Uncle Wensleydale was right. Some human person had at last invented a mousetrap that not even a house mouse could find a way of springing.

They considered trying to push it off the bookcase, but Uncle Wensleydale said he feared it was too heavy for them, and too dangerous. Getting it over the wrinkles in the sheet might spring it and there was no good way of getting a grip on it except by taking hold of the jaws. It would be easy to lose a hand. They looked at it gloomily for a long time.

Meanwhile Smalleata had found her nose wrinkling

with an instinct to sneeze. It was the smell of mothballs that Raffles had earlier told her the human people put in the case to keep mice from the books. A few were scattered over the top, round white balls with a tendency to glitter in the light. For some reason she was never able afterwards to think of, she picked one up, offensive as the smell of it was. It was not heavy to lift, though it felt solid in her hands. And then the idea came to her.

"Raffles," she said, "couldn't I throw this at the pan and spring it that way?"

Without waiting she reached back her arm and brought it forward in an overhand pitch. The mothball flew just above the pan. But Raffles saw at once how possible it might be. He picked up another mothball and let fly. It too went over.

"Take turns, take turns!" Uncle Wensleydale shouted suddenly as the young mice reached for more mothballs. He had picked out one for himself. He was obviously in a state of great excitement.

Setting his feet firmly, he held the ball out at arm's length, sighting at the pan. Then he drew back, and threw, and the ball went fair to the mark. There was a snap. The upper jaw came down, the teeth meshed with the lower jaw. The mothball had vanished.

"I wonder what some human person will make of that next spring," he said. "A trap that eats mothballs." He chuckled, then turned to Smalleata.

"That was a marvelous idea. I ought to have let you throw to spring it, and if we ever find another trap like it, that's what I'll do."

"Yes," Raffles said. "You're right, Uncle Wensleydale.

She's too good a mouse not to be a member of our family. I am going to make home with her, and Uncle, will you come soon to visit her people? They would like to meet you."

"They're the field mice upstairs?"

"Yes," said Raffles.

"It will be a pleasure, my dear. We shall call tomorrow."

22

FOR QUITE A WHILE that night Smalleata lay awake, her thoughts full of everything she had done during the day. Not only because of the springing of the traps, including the last new one, but for the wonderful sense of having made the house safe for all other mice. Even the young careless ones could go anywhere now without a fear of being caught in a trap. Nor because Uncle Wensleydale had said before they parted that there were only the weasels to be afraid of now until the snow came deep enough to cover the foundations of the house and make it really into a castle in which the mice could feel safe from all other animals. But mainly because of the call next day that Uncle Wensleydale was coming to make. What would her family think of Raffles's uncle? She thought she would *never* get to sleep, and when she finally did so, it seemed only a second before the stirrings of her mother and sisters told her that tomorrow had already come.

Smalleata's mother was turning out the house. On even ordinary days she was a bustling sort of mouse, but today, with this young house mouse's family coming to call, she was determined to have her house in such a perfect state that these house mice would have to feel impressed. In that way she would be able to look down on them with no feeling of conscience.

She had Smalleata's sisters and, as soon as she was awake, Smalleata too, flying about, straightening this and hiding that until the air in the house was like a mist of dusty fluff, and Smalleata began sneezing. Only then did her mother relax and say, "We had better let the air clear, I think. Luckily there's just time."

Smalleata went out into the space between the floor joists to see other families busy round their houses. But Uncle Stilton was sitting beside his, back propped against the joist and his legs crossed, quite relaxed. He had obviously done not a thing to his place, and yet with its red roof it had an air the other houses didn't have.

"That mouse," exclaimed Smalleata's mother. "No one should be allowed to stay a bachelor. So sloppy!"

Smalleata didn't think he looked sloppy at all, and she had a sudden qualm to think of his portly and distinguished figure confronting little stooped Uncle Wensleydale in his drab gray front. What would the other field mice think when they met Raffles and his family?

She needn't have worried. It all went off very well from the moment the first field mice in the farther alleys came out of their houses to meet the house mice. There was a continual scurrying and flurry of high-pitched mouse voices. The sound grew louder as it came nearer, and Smalleata held her breath when she saw Uncle Wensleydale's head appearing in the entrance to their street. Raffles was right behind him, and both had bags in their hands. Behind them was Raffles's mother, looking as vague as she had in the sunlight on the kitchen table. And then came a collection of house mice of all ages. It was a mouse gathering such as had never taken place in the house before.

Uncle Wensleydale said as much as he presented his bag to Uncle Stilton. "It's a pleasure," he said, "for us house mice to welcome so fine a colony of field mice as you are."

"The pleasure is mutual," Uncle Stilton replied in a courtly way. "And I've heard a great deal about your cleverness, sir, from Smalleata."

Uncle Wensleydale grinned and looked to one side, and to relieve his embarrassment, Uncle Stilton opened the bag and pulled out a small square cracker that smelled of cheese. He nibbled it and wiggled his whiskers in a fast, quivery way.

"Excellent," he said. "Excellent! Very tangy!"

"I'm glad you like it," said Uncle Wensleydale. "We were very well satisfied when the human people switched to this brand. 'Eaton's Cheese Cocktail Snacks.'"

"Cocktail," Uncle Stilton said with a laugh. "The only one I ever saw was on the end of a white rooster who came up across our meadow, and Reagan Ready made short work of him, I can tell you."

"I expect he must have. I don't know why human people call the drink they take before dinner a cocktail and the one after a highball," said Uncle Wensleydale. "I've watched them at it and all I can tell is that both things make them noisier. They make noise enough round the house as it is."

"A terrible clattery-bang all day long," said Raffles's mother.

"It must be very trying," agreed Smalleata's mother. She opened the package Raffles had brought as his mother's gift to her. It contained sesame seeds, which she had tasted only once in her life but regarded as an exceptional delicacy. From that point on she considered Raffles's mother to be a very ladylike person in spite of her singular vagueness of manner, and she then quite happily brought up the young people's hopes of making home together.

"*Are* they?" exclaimed Raffles's mother in a faraway voice. "I'd no idea. Or maybe I've forgotten. But anyway I let Wensleydale make all the decisions for the family. So much easier in the long run. And saves argument."

"Then why don't we go out and speak to him and Stilton," Smalleata's mother suggested. Not that she would have dreamed of leaving any decision affecting her own life to any male mouse, but more to make things easy for her new friend.

They found the two old mice sitting with their backs against the joist, the bag of cocktail snacks between them from which each in turn would fish a snack. They greeted the two mothers amiably without making any move to get up.

"We came," Smalleata's mother began, "to discuss this business of Smalleata and Raffles wanting to make home."

"Nothing to discuss. Wensleydale and I've settled it already," Uncle Stilton said. "Actually he suggested it, but in my opinion it's an admirable idea."

The lady mice looked inquiringly at Uncle Wensleydale. He looked faintly anxious.

"Well," he said, taking his right side-whiskers in his hand and stroking the length of them so that not only was his arm at full stretch but the whiskers were curved back like a bow (he had unusually luxuriant whiskers for a house mouse). "Well," he repeated, letting his whiskers snap out straight and stiff, "there are one or two points I presented to Stilton for his consideration, and it is very gratifying to have him agree with my point of view regarding them."

He helped himself to another snack, and Smalleata's mother noticed a slight look of apprehension in Uncle Stilton's eyes.

"Point one," said Uncle Wensleydale, after a nibble. "We are now in mid-December. This is the month we have to be wary of weasels coming into the house. By the end of the year, though, the way it's snowing, the snow ought to cover the house foundations and sills, so there will be no way for the weasels to get in, and from then on the house will be safe for any mouse anywhere."

He nibbled again.

"Point two," he went on, "is that after the turn of the year we always have a visit from the Gogie. He is like a little man but he lives in the brook. Once every winter he pays us a visit, not so much to see us, but to turn on the TV box so he can watch the great President, Abraham Lyndon, make his speech on the State of the Human Union. But all we house mice always watch it with him, and he explains what the President is saying, and what he says he has in mind. It's just as well, even for mice, to hear what any human person thinks he's going to do, even though he generally does something else."

Absentmindedly he reached for another cocktail snack, and equally absentmindedly Uncle Stilton moved the bag out of Uncle Wensleydale's reach as he fished one out for himself.

"And now, point three," said Uncle Wensleydale. "It occurred to me when Raffles told me what he and Smalleata had in mind that this would be an ideal chance to celebrate their making home. As far as I can recall, there has never been such a thing before — a house mouse and a field mouse making home together. So this first time ought to be a great occasion. We'll have the TV party, and then the young can dance or play the stair game, after which we'll send them off. It will be an honor," he said formally to Uncle Stilton, "if all you field mice will join in with us."

Though Uncle Wensleydale seemed to Smalleata to have taken a great many words to say what he had to say — it sounded in fact as if he were practicing to make a speech — she thought his plan sounded very exciting; and Uncle Stilton and the two mothers evidently approved also. All of a sudden she felt she could hardly wait for the new year to come, and when she looked at Raffles, she saw that he felt the same way.

23

"I CAME HERE by accident last summer," said Raffles, looking round. "And I thought at the time it might be a good place for a mouse to make home in."

The spot he had brought her to was over the room in which the human people, when they were in the house, left toast crumbs in the morning, and the joist behind their backs was tight against the main chimney, into which both furnaces fed, so that she had noticed at once that it was warmer than the rest of the house (outside of the cellar) and also drier. The only entrance to the space was through a slanted knothole near the far end of the joist. And now as she got her directions sorted out, Small-eata realized that the far end was right at the partition that separated the room below from the storage closet in which they had first sprung the traps and where all the jellies, jams, and wine were stored. It came into her mind that somehow, sometime, this might well be to the advantage of mice having a home so handy by.

From the space between the next two joists there were several ways to get down into the kitchen and cellar or across the upper ceiling to all the rest of the house, including the settlement the field mice had made. It seemed to her an ideal place; she loved the sense they would have of being off alone.

"It would be beautiful here," she said to Raffles, meaning every word, and they decided then and there that this was the time to begin building their house.

It was so different from building a house on the pine hill. There, nature was the same as it had been even before Uncle Stilton's birth — whenever that ancient event had taken place. Milkweed grew there then and milkweed grew now. In fact many kinds of grass had been introduced into the field that had not grown there years before and many were better for nest-making. But here in the house it was much harder to find things to build a house with.

It was mainly because of the human people. The way they put camphor balls among the books, for instance. Smalleata had discovered they were harmless to mice, and even useful for springing traps, but she would never have brought book paper smelling like camphor into her home. She did not believe it would be healthful for babies. Nor was there any wallpaper, like Uncle Stilton's red roof, left in the attic. They had to rely almost entirely on a stack of folded newspapers in a cupboard in the pantry where all the plates and glasses were.

This of course was easy for them to get at. The house mice had always taken pains to keep a way open into that cupboard. So it did not take many days for them to carry enough long shreds up between the walls and across to their own place next the chimney.

They first made a thick pad of it for a floor, so none of the laths and lumps of plaster could be felt through it. Then they made a mound over it, oval shaped and rising towards the rear, because Smalleata said she wanted to have her nest as far as possible from the entrance. Perhaps she was thinking of her home under the pine roots, but Raffles in any case thought it an excellent and original plan.

Some of the newspapers they tore up had pictures in colors and these they saved for the roof so that their house had a gay and lively appearance, if not as elegant as Uncle Stilton's solid red roof. But they thought it very beautiful and sometimes sat down together just to look at it.

It was in one of these moments that Smalleata told Raffles her idea of using toilet paper for the lining.

He agreed that it would be wonderful if they could only get hold of some. But the human people always put it away in tightly covered tin barrels.

"It must be much more valuable to them than newspaper and books," he said.

"But," cried Smalleata, "I saw it up on the wall in all the bathrooms."

"I know it's there, but how could I get at it? The wall's too slippery to climb," Raffles said, but seeing the anxious longing in her eyes, he determined to find *some* way of getting at the rolls on the walls. However, to reassure her now, he said that it was the house mouse custom (as it was) to line their nests the day they went off to make home in it together. In other words they would have to wait till the end of the party Uncle Wensleydale had dreamed up, which seemed to them a very long way off.

24

I<small>T WAS NOT</small> really, of course. Every day Uncle Wensleydale insisted on checking on the depth of snow round the house. As the days got shorter and the nights longer, he seemed to become more nervous and at times was almost jittery in his movements. Either he made the check himself, going down to the driveway, or Raffles went, which naturally now meant Smalleata, too.

It was snowing nearly every day, and the space beneath the driveway doors had filled, with a small drift coming in across the floor. After that they would go here and there to look out through chinks where the foundation blocks had tilted, leaving narrow spaces under the sills. Though it was a squeeze getting through some of them enough to poke one's head outdoors, Raffles managed it and could report the level of snow getting steadily deeper.

But Uncle Wensleydale became increasingly impatient. Whenever it was snowing he insisted on checks being made twice a day, and all round the house. On one of these, Raffles and Smalleata went across the laundry ceiling to look out beside the privy over the brook. It was still snowing softly, and on the bank of the brook they saw tracks approaching the base of the privy and snow tossed out fanwise, where someone had dug it to get under and in.

When they had scrabbled down the wall and stood by the tracks in the snow, Smalleata realized that this was the first time she had been outside the house in months; and she felt strange. The wind blowing over the snow was colder than she had ever known, and the outdoor sounds alarmed her. She kept looking everywhere to be sure they were safe.

"I'm already becoming a house mouse," she said to herself, but then when she looked at Raffles, he seemed perfectly unconcerned. He was examining the footprints in the snow.

The front ones looked like long-fingered hands and those behind had little marks like the heel prints of old Honeysuckle, though they were very much smaller than any bear's. The animal, whoever it was, had had to push to get itself under the bottom of the privy and had left a few brownish-gray hairs in the rough edge of the wood.

Raffles looked at them for a while. Then he said, "I'm going to go in and see where it went."

Naturally, he had no difficulty getting in, but at least, thought Smalleata, he was cautious, putting only his nose and whiskers through till he could see what was inside.

"Whatever it is has climbed up into the house," he told her. "But we can't follow it because of the board with the hole in it."

So he led the way back up the foundation stones and up inside the outer wall of the laundry and across over the ceiling till they were between the floor joists that looked down into the privy from above. There was nothing to see there, but a strange sourish smell, not unpleasant, like the edge of some of the pickle jars stored in the closet, filled the air. Smalleata was reminded a little of the smell old Honeysuckle left behind, but then she remembered another time, she couldn't think when . . .

And Raffles began to say, "It must be the . . ."

At the same time there was a scuffling sound behind them; the faint light at the far end of the alley was blocked out; and out of the darkness they could hear a large shape scuffling quickly towards them. Neither of them could move, until the shape came near enough their open end for them to see that whatever it was filled the entire space. It had to crawl, because its back scraped so tight against the floor boards above it.

Raffles, in a rather shaky voice, finished his sentence. "It must be the raccoon."

"Yes," said the animal in a rasping, unpleasant voice.

In time, Smalleata was to learn that the raccoon had a note for its young, as soft and sweet as a drowsy bird's. But now she was not feeling at all friendly. Nor did she look friendly with her heavy teeth and the narrow muzzle with snarling lips; and across her face a mask of black through which her small eyes blazed and glittered.

"Listen to me, you little mice," she said. "This is *my* home now. And I don't like mice, or anyone else, to come in here. If I find you here next May when my babies are born, I'll kill you. I eat mice quite often," she added ominously.

"We won't," Raffles promised, politely. Smalleata saw that now that he had recovered his surprise he was not at all alarmed, and suddenly she realized that in this close space the raccoon could never catch them. Raffles, however, did not let on that he knew. He said, in the same polite voice: "I hope you will be comfortable here."

"It's a little crowded for me," the raccoon confessed. "But that means that after my babies are born their father won't be able to get in and eat them. Even if he managed to squeeze his way up here," she added, with a

little sniff rather like a sneeze, "the babies could run away from him. The way you could from me."

Raffles grinned at her, and she grinned back, but Small-eata, looking at their teeth, thought their expressions were not at all alike.

"Anyway," Raffles went on, "if we get a little more snow, the house will be fine and safe. All we worry about now are the weasels getting in before the snow covers the foundations. Have you seen any sign of them?"

"Yes, I saw them yesterday down at the mouth of the

brook," the raccoon said. "There were four of them, an older pair and two young ones. I myself am not afraid of weasels, though they are nasty things to kill. They have no fear at all. But I can see why you would be anxious. They are particularly fond of killing mice."

"Did you see which way they went?"

"They were going along the riverbank," replied the raccoon. "They were hard to see, all white, running in the snow. I might not have seen them at all if the biggest one hadn't turned to look at me with his red eyes."

"Well," said Raffles, "my Uncle Wensleydale says it's going to snow tonight. And if it covers the bottom of the house we don't need to worry. Weasels can't chew into wood the way we can."

"No," said the raccoon, beginning to sound a bit bored with the conversation. "They can't do that."

Raffles caught the note in her voice and quickly said good-bye, and he and Smalleata retreated into the privy.

Through the small window in the back of it they could look out across the brook to the bushes and the meadow beyond.

"Look," he cried, "it's snowing already. And snowing harder every minute."

That meant the weasels would not trouble them, and when they had climbed up into the entrance to another alley between the ceiling joists, Smalleata raced after him full of a wonderful feeling of joy.

They crossed the ceiling over the driveway, which was not roomy enough to let the raccoon through, so they did not have to think of her any longer, and they came out on top of the broad foundation wall and started along it for the room where all the jars had been broken by the rats. There was no more glass in the cellar to be smashed, but just the same the Rockendollar boys were having a roughhouse all over the floor and the woodpile. The idea seemed to be to gang up in pursuit of one and when he climbed up on the wood to escape, to throw him bodily off it. If he got up limping, the others would laugh at the top of their raucous voices.

Only two had not joined the game. One, naturally enough, was old Mr. Rockendollar himself. He was sitting with his back against the box of the main furnace, looking on through half-closed eyes. The other was the fattest of the young rats, Nussbaum, who was up on one of the pair of oil tanks, peering at the gauge with his eyes only an inch from the glass, for he was very nearsighted.

As Smalleata and Raffles slipped along so as not to attract attention, they heard him muttering, with a curious chittering of his teeth, "No more oil. Almost no more oil." But at the time it meant nothing to them.

25

THAT EVENING, after they had stopped to see Uncle Wensleydale for a moment and dropped in on Smalleata's mother and Uncle Stilton, they went up to the attic. When they looked out the window they saw that the snow was driving much harder.

"Almost a blizzard," Raffles said.

The light had nearly gone. All they could see was the white of the snow and the black branches of the pine trees moving up and down on the wind. Behind them the attic was getting very dark; but suddenly back there they heard a scampering of feet; and then the sound of soft, gentle busy voices, and Smalleata went back to see what was going on.

Almost at once she met an animal she had never seen. It was like a squirrel, only a soft gray brown with a pearly gray front rather like her own, and the most beautiful eyes she had ever seen.

"Who are you?" the squirrel asked Smalleata.

"My name is Smalleata. I'm a field mouse and we're spending the winter here. Only," she added with a catch in her voice, "*I'm* going to live here forever. With Raffles," and she pointed to him back at the window.

The squirrel looked at him so gently that Smalleata was encouraged to ask, "Are you a squirrel? You look like one but not like any one I ever saw."

"We are flying squirrels," replied the squirrel. "And we come every winter, once the snow begins to get deep. Then we leave for the woods in the spring."

"That's just what we do, too," said Smalleata, before she remembered. "Or almost all of us do. But how do you fly? You have no wings."

The squirrel's eyes twinkled.

"Perhaps we shouldn't really call it flying," she admitted. "But look at Misty up there on the cupboard. She's just going to take some cherrystones to put away in her house."

On the corner of the cupboard another squirrel crouched. Suddenly she sprang out with all her might. She stretched out all four legs and a fold of skin straightened out between each front and hind leg. She came swooping down and Smalleata held her breath, thinking she would surely smash into the floor. But at the last moment she swooped up and just caught the bottom of an old golf bag that had been hung high from a nail near the peak where two rafters joined. As soon as she had hold of it she climbed quickly up it to the pocket where long ago some old golfer had carried his golf balls and quickly emptied the cherrystones from her cheek pouches into it.

"We keep our food in the pockets but we sleep down at the bottom of the bags. It's very snug and warm down there, and nothing can get at us," explained the flying squirrel.

There were two other golf bags and for a while Smalleata watched the flying squirrels making them ready for the winter. It was a wonderful sight, with all of them swooping back and forth about their business. She wished for a moment that she was built with a flap of skin between her legs, but then she realized that she would not have been a field mouse and about to make home with a house mouse. She looked for Raffles, but he was still watching the snow through the window. It was coming down harder than ever.

26

IN THE MORNING a wave of rejoicing ran through the two colonies of mice. Snow had drifted high against the foundations of the house. When they went up to the attic and looked from the window, Smalleata and Raffles looked out on a brand-new world. More than two feet of snow had fallen overnight. The branches of the pines, carrying great white burdens of it, nearly touched the ground. The bridge across the brook was filled to the top of its railings.

The snow had brought a new chill into the attic, but the bright sunlight that shone through the window made it a comfortable place. Behind them they could hear the flying squirrels beginning to stir and the soft thuds of their feet as they lit on the floor after jumping from the mouths of their golf bags. One or two of them came to look out of the window, too, and Smalleata thought how pleasant it was to have such nice and gentle animals for their neighbors in the attic. To have had the Rockendollars shouting and thumping overhead in their wild games would have been unbearable.

All of a sudden, beyond the bridge, they heard the farmer's caterpillar tractor clanking along the drive. He was plowing the driveway with a big blade in front which pushed up a high bank of the new fluffy snow and left the driveway like a smooth white ditch between high banks. The tractor was painted orange; in the frosty air its exhaust pipe made little white rings that floated straight up, and sometimes the pipe the farmer was smoking made a ring, also. He had on a bright red coat. In spite of the squeaking and creaking and clatter of the tracks on the cold snow, Smalleata thought it would be wonderful to drive a machine like that and shove the snow away from one, anywhere one wanted to go. She could just imagine Uncle Stilton plowing a way for them down from the hill to the house. Reagan Ready would have had to get out of their way all right. Not even old Honeysuckle could have argued with the tractor.

It went on past the house, turning the corner and going on down the drive with the farmer still smoking his pipe until they could not hear it. Then after a while it came back, throwing the snow to the other side of the drive, so in the two trips the farmer had made a wide open road, big enough for an automobile or even a truck to come through. And as a matter of fact, a few minutes later a truck did come up the drive and stop in front of the bridge.

The truck had a long round body painted red, with large white letters along its side that said ADIRONDACK OIL & FUEL CORP. The mice and flying squirrels had no idea of what that meant, of course; but Raffles suddenly felt uneasy. He saw the driver get down from the truck and start to shout at someone across the brook. Then the farmer came back into view, walking with a shovel on his shoulder, and he was shouting back at the truck driver. Every time they opened their mouths clouds of steam came out along with whatever they were saying.

Then, after they had talked back and forth for quite a while, the farmer began to dig a path through the snow towards the house. He came straight for a while, but then he slanted his direction for the driveway. Meanwhile the truck driver had gone to the back of his truck and opened a door. Inside was a heavy coiled black hose with a big nozzle, which he put on his shoulder. He followed the farmer down the narrow snowy path, with the hose unwinding behind him. Pretty soon they disappeared; but Raffles realized all at once that they must have opened the driveway doors. And as a matter of fact, they always preferred filling the oil tanks in the warmth of the cellar to standing around in the cold outside the house, feeding the oil slowly through the long outside pipes. It was much more comfortable for them in the cellar, but Raffles was now sure that the house was once more open to the weasels.

He did not say anything to Smalleata, but when at last the two men reappeared, bringing the hose and shovel, and had spent several minutes more talking beside the truck, and then gone across the brook to fill the farmhouse tank, he told her that he had to go down to the cellar. She wanted to go with him, but if what he dreaded had really happened, he did not want her to see it, so he said he would meet her in a few minutes at Uncle Stilton's house.

27

W HEN he reached the driveway, his worst fears were confirmed. The snow had been shoveled right away from one of the driveway doors and now the sun was streaming under it. The house once again was open to weasels or any other marauding animal small enough to squeeze under the door.

He felt very sober as he reentered the cellar. The Rockendollars seemed not to realize what had happened. Some of the boys were frolicking back of the furnaces; old Mr. Rockendollar sat on a covered trash barrel contentedly feeling of his nostrils with two fingers of one hand; and Nussbaum was on top of the oil tank examining the gauge and exclaiming, "Full up. Right to the top. Oodles of oil," with great satisfaction. He grinned as Raffles went by without apparently a thought of what it could mean.

Raffles quickly made his way to Uncle Wensleydale to explain what had happened. The old mouse was in the preserve closet, tinkering hopefully with the top of a jar of raspberry jam. He listened to what Raffles had to tell him; then he slipped down off the jar.

"We'll have to round up our people," he said. "They've scattered all over the house since the snow came."

"Yes," Raffles said, "but I'm thinking of the field mice, too. They've got themselves a good place with only one way the weasels can get in, but they don't know anything about plugging holes."

"Well, I suppose we'll have to see to them, too," Uncle Wensleydale said with a sigh. He told Raffles to go up and warn Stilton and said he would be along in due course with material for plugging the knothole that opened the way into the field mouse settlement. Meanwhile other young house mice could carry the alarm all through the house.

Uncle Stilton faced the situation with his usual determination. He saw at once that the crux of the situation was the first entrance hole near the chimney.

"There are nails and broken glass at the bottom of the shaft next the one we use coming up from the cellar," he said. "Maybe we could use that to plug our doorway."

"Weasels couldn't bite through broken glass," Raffles agreed tactfully. "But it might be hard to wedge it in tight enough so the weasels could not pull it out. They don't care a thing about cutting themselves."

Uncle Stilton understood how that might be, but he insisted on going to the door to study it himself. All his life he had been a mouse of action and the situation now confronting them was not to be solved by sitting still.

"What do you house mice do about this?" he asked as they made their way towards the crucial entrance.

By now all the other field mice knew the danger. Some watched anxiously as Uncle Stilton, Raffles, and Small-eata went by, but others fell in behind them, and soon a small group of them gathered at the entrance.

They had been there only a minute when the sound of

mice climbing up from the cellar reached them. Uncle Wensleydale, followed by a dozen or so house mice, climbed up out of the shaft.

"Glad to see you're all right, Stilton," he said. "Though I don't expect the weasels will show up before twilight." The younger mice behind him were carrying cylinders of different sizes of what was apparently a very light material. Most had a dull red stain.

"Wine corks," Uncle Wensleydale said brusquely. "I've made a habit of collecting them. Of course, your situation is a bit awkward because we'll have to shove the cork in from outside. If the cork was small enough to go through to your side, it wouldn't plug the hole."

"I can see that," Uncle Stilton said. "You'll have to close us in. But as soon as this business is over, I shall engineer cutting a large enough hole to get the proper size corks into our place, and then find another way to plug it permanently."

"Good idea," Uncle Wensleydale said briefly. "You'd better get in now."

As soon as all the field mice had retired to their own side of the joist, he began selecting corks. He soon found one that fitted in snug and when pushed hard was a little deeper than the face of the joist.

"I'll bring you word when it's safe to come out," he shouted; but his voice sounded thin and rather far away to the field mice on the far side. "You can push it out from your side then."

"Yes," said Raffles. "And the weasels can't get at it with their hands, and they haven't got the teeth for chewing wood."

A wave of happiness swept Smalleata's heart. She hadn't expected Raffles to stay with them.

But all he did was grin at her, perhaps a little bashfully; and Uncle Stilton said, "It's certainly very kind of your relations to look out for us, Raffles. But after this I'll see to it we stand on our own feet."

28

IT FELT strange to be shut in. The rest of the house suddenly seemed like a separate world, far away. She went back with Raffles and Uncle Stilton to their own street and they sat together outside Uncle Stilton's house. Some mice came by to ask Uncle Stilton whether he really thought the weasels would come.

"How should I know?" Uncle Stilton asked testily; but he got even more cross when some young male mice suggested that it was all a big bugaboo started by the house mice as a sort of joke. He spoke his mind to them rather sharply and then picked out two or three stout mice to act as a guard over the corked hole.

Smalleata's mother was the most trying of all, coming again and again to ask, "Do you think we are really safe, Stilton?"

Smalleata saw that it was going to be a long night; and it was not even twilight yet. They waited together and Uncle Stilton reminisced about his early life in England. He had tenanted a small country inn, famous for its cheese, and having a partiality for Stilton cheese, had gradually acquired an aroma from which he had got his name. He had made the mistake, early one morning, of climbing into a suitcase in which a human guest had put away a section of Stilton to bring home. He had been closed in and come all the way to America by air — landing in Boston at a dingy airport named Logan, in which, it being Boston summer at its hottest and muggiest, even the customs inspectors had been logier than usual. There had been a bit of a scene, he recalled, when the inspector reached into the suitcase. Four uniformed men had pursued him to the taxi stand, but he had leaped into one just as the door was closing and crawled into the passenger's overcoat pocket. It turned out to be the pocket of the human person who lived in this house, which was how he had come to live here.

Smalleata had heard the story a good many times before, but Raffles looked very interested and asked questions about the sensations of flight.

"In my case," said Uncle Stilton, "it was an uninterrupted six-hour banquet of cheese. I shall never forget the experience."

And somehow, for Smalleata, the familiarity of the story was comforting.

In the late afternoon they were aware of the wind blowing strongly from the north. Then about sunset the wind died away. It must be getting very cold outside, for they could hear the timbers of the house creaking from time to time.

"I should think we would have northern lights tonight," Uncle Stilton said; but of course there was no way for them to go and see. Smalleata would have loved to climb to the attic window and watch the long wavering streamers of light reaching out across the sky, she had heard Uncle Stilton describe them so often. But instead there was nothing she could do but try to appear interested in his reminiscences; and then she realized that he was telling them to keep her mind off what might be going to happen beyond the corked door. She thought again what a dear old person he really was and wondered if Stilton cheese might not smell as he did now, rich, slightly oily, and very mouse. To be close to him was reassuring and soothing. She had almost dropped asleep when Raffles stirred and suddenly sat up.

"Listen," he whispered. "I think I hear something."

Smalleata could hear nothing at all. Then it came to her that this itself was very strange. Usually the house was full of sounds, even if tiny ones in moments deep in the night or at noon. Somewhere a mouse might be stirring, or a small twig from one of the pines would tap the roof. But now she heard no sounds at all. It was as if every mouse like herself was straining to listen, as if the house itself was listening for something.

Then far below she heard a thin cry.

"That's one of the Rockendollar boys," whispered Raffles. "Come on. I want to listen by the door."

But when they reached the corked doorway, they found they could hear more clearly what was happening in the cellar by listening at the head of the shaft next the chimney one which provided the route from cellar to attic. There was no hole leading into it below, for which they now said silent blessings, but through the crack above the sill sounds from the cellar came clearly. Somebody was screaming.

He was screaming and running, for the voice came first loud and then dimly and then again loud.

"It's one of the Rockendollars," Raffles said in a shaky voice. "The weasels are after him."

A rat can move very fast when he wants to, and when he knows corners to dodge around he is very hard to catch. But weasels, once the will to kill gets hold of them, can run forever. And they move as quickly as any animal their size on earth.

The mice at the edge of the shaft heard the rat stop at last to fight; but fierce as the rat was he could not match the deadly swift spring of the weasel. They heard his last yell choked off, and silence welled up through the darkness like fear itself. Through it they suddenly heard the sharp chattering of teeth.

It was old Mr. Rockendollar. He must be cornered somewhere with one or two of the weasels coming at him. And suddenly that sound, too, stopped.

Smalleata had always shuddered when she came close to one of the Rockendollars. Now she felt only pity for them. She wondered if they were all dead. But presently she and the other listening mice huddled together at the mouth of the shaft heard the sound of climbing toenails in the next chimney shaft. Someone was climbing as fast and silently as he could.

He was halfway up when they heard the sound of two or three more animals swarming up behind. The first climber let out a shriek. They could hear his feet scrabbling with redoubled speed. He kept on yelling; as if that would do any good. He was hauling himself out of the shaft, just outside the corked door. And then Smalleata heard a sharp hissing sound.

In all her life afterwards she never heard another sound that sent the same chill straight to her heart. She thought it would stop beating. The hiss came again, and then a second animal made the same sound, and the rat outside turned at the edge of the shaft to fight. He was still shrieking with terror, but he knew he had to fight.

"It's Nussbaum Rockendollar," Raffles said in a chilled small voice.

They heard him shriek again and the sound of terribly quick feet going at him. Then his voice stopped. There was threshing and suddenly bodies were tumbling down the shaft and everything was still.

"They killed him," Uncle Stilton said. "They had him before he fell, and weasels never let go once they have your throat. Not till you, or they, are dead."

There was no other sound for a long time, though all the field mice huddled together by the corked door. Twice before dawn they heard the passage of weasels, racing between the outside joists or running through the attic. They knew they were the weasels by the hisses they let out. They were still savage and looking for animals to kill.

"They are more terrible than even human persons," Uncle Stilton said. "They go mad, without really being mad, and they kill a great many more things than they ever need or use."

Obviously they could smell where mice had been and were looking for their homes. Smalleata thought how terrible it would have been if they had been living in their colony of tunnels under the pine hill. They had no way of shutting out such creatures there. If it had not been for the house mice, particularly Uncle Wensleydale, they might now all be dead.

It was long after day when a voice called from outside the corked door. Uncle Wensleydale was as dry as ever, but even he sounded shaken.

"They've gone," he said. "Push the door through, Raffles."

As the cork popped out they saw his thin and troubled old face looking at them.

"Are your people all all right?" asked Uncle Stilton.

Wensleydale nodded.

"But they killed old Rockendollar and Nussbaum and three of the boys. Only two got away. They've gone out through the driveway and down the road and when I went out to look at their tracks, the weasel tracks were following them."

Smalleata shivered.

"But," said Uncle Wensleydale. "It's begun to snow."

She and Raffles went straight up to the attic window. It really was snowing again, and steadily it snowed harder with a cold wind from the north. It was the most beautiful sight she had ever seen.

29

TOWARDS NOON they went down to the cellar. Several mice, working under the direction of Uncle Stilton and Uncle Wensleydale, had dragged the body of Nussbaum Rockendollar out of the shaft. It lay now on the floor of the room with the jars he had helped break, and beside him, its jaws locked in his throat, was the body of one of the weasels, whose back must have been broken by the long fall.

He was all white, with a very short dense coat, but what surprised Smalleata was how slender his body was. He could have entered any hole big enough for her. His eyes were closed so she could not see whether they were red, as the raccoon had described them; but she could well believe they had been for even dead he looked vicious and merciless. Poor Nussbaum Rockendollar! It was hard to grasp that anyone so riotous and noisy could be so still. He made no sound even while the mice dragged him through the cellar to the driveway. When the farmer found him there, he would suppose that that was where the weasels had overtaken him. He might wonder why the weasel was dead, but it would not trouble him. He liked neither weasels nor rats—nor mice, when it came to that, said Uncle Wensleydale.

The weasels did not come back. The snow that had begun to fall that night kept on for three days and ev-

erything outside the attic window glistened white. The house was now truly a safe place and Smalleata, as mice do, soon forgot that terrible night and thought only about the TV party and her making home with Raffles.

With the ending of the old year it was the main subject of conversation among the mice. Smalleata's mother and Raffles's mother joined forces to plan for special food to have after the TV show, but Raffles's mother was too vague to be much help and kept suggesting particular things that could only be procured out of doors in the middle of summer. Actually, it was Uncle Stilton and Uncle Wensleydale who planned the feast, which required a remarkable amount of sampling on their part and caused Raffles to worry a little about whether there would be anything left to eat at all.

But he needn't have worried. Uncle Wensleydale dipped into secret stores and Uncle Stilton proved to have concealed in his red-roofed house a great many more delicacies than he could ever have brought in his pack-sack. No one knew how he had got hold of them, and he naturally was the last person to tell.

On the afternoon before the party the two old mice enlisted the help of various others, including the two mothers, though Raffles's mother wasn't of much use except to clasp her hands in admiration. Uncle Stilton had decided that the sideboard across from the table in the dining room would be ideal for the buffet. There was plenty of room to arrange the food and the older mice could look down on those dancing on the table. They piled their heaps of seeds and cereal at the base of each of the two decanters till they made an elaborate and tempting show.

Between the decanters was a silver cruet stand with a handle that arched out of two tiny calla lillies. It had five cutglass flasks. One was for salt, and another for mustard, and both had silver tops, and the other three held respectively cider and wine vinegar and olive oil. Raffles's mother thought it an extremely beautiful piece and Uncle Stilton admitted that it had a certain elegance. But it would be nice, he thought, if something could be done to give it a festive air.

At that point Raffles, who had been keeping himself in the background, spoke up.

"If nobody minds, I'd like to decorate it myself," he said.

Uncle Stilton looked as if he didn't much approve of anyone else taking a role in the arrangements he had been supervising with so much authority, but Uncle Wensleydale said he thought it was a good idea. "After all," he commented, "Raffles is one of the interested parties." And after that Uncle Stilton could hardly raise further objections.

Smalleata wanted to help him, but Raffles said, no, his decoration was to surprise her, and suddenly he had disappeared. After a while, when Uncle Stilton's preparations were completed and he had appointed several reliable mice to guard the buffet, even from the *oldest* and *most respectable* mice, he emphasized in obvious reference to Uncle Wensleydale's absentminded way of putting out a hand and helping himself to a mouthful of this or that, she decided to go up to her own place for a rest before the party started.

30

WHEN SHE WOKE the sun had set. She went up to
the attic and looked from the window. The snow had
stopped and the night was completely clear; but while she
looked out a finger of pale green light reached out across
the sky and faded away. But then came another, and one
whiter, and then one of a soft rosy color, and one of violet,
and more of green and almost blue, until the whole sky
was alive with pulsing shafts of colored light and the
night outside seemed nearly as bright as day.

"Northern lights," she breathed. "For my party night.
For *Raffles's* and my party night!"

All of a sudden she felt she had to find him and raced
through the attic and then down the stairs, taking two or
even three steps at a time. She felt reckless and safe, as if
she had wings, even on the bottom floor as she ran into
the dining room.

The whole room was aglow with the bright sky; and
the change of colors made it almost dreamlike. She looked
up at the sideboard and saw that Uncle Stilton had returned to it, possibly with a view of protecting the
eatables of the buffet from Uncle Wensleydale, though
possibly with the idea of a little last minute, judicious
sampling on his own part. And then she saw the caster
stand. It had been festooned with twisted lengths of

white soft paper till it looked as beautiful as one of the snowladen pines outside. She caught her breath, then climbed the chair beside the sideboard and jumped onto the top. Raffles was just finishing tucking the last bits in at the foot of the stand.

"Raffles!" she cried. "It's beautiful. I never saw anything so beautiful. It's *toilet* paper!"

He glanced at her and then in a self-conscious way back at his snow tree.

"I found a way to get it," he said. "We can get all we want at the end of the party, to line our house."

"Oh, where?" she asked.

But he wouldn't say; and just then Uncle Wensleydale reappeared to announce that the time had come to watch the TV. Mr. Gogie, he said, was on his way.

It was, of course, a crucial moment as far as the buffet went, for everyone wanted to see the President describe the State of the Human Union. But Uncle Stilton had worked it all out. He sent everyone off the sideboard, except himself, while Uncle Wensleydale assembled them in the living room.

The house mice came in troops and families from the kitchen and pantry, but the field mice came all in a single body down the stairs and marched along the hall. They seemed a bit stiff and embarrassed, for none of them had ever been to a TV party before, and some looked a little anxious, not knowing what it would be like to see a human person talking at one out of a box, especially such a large box.

However, to Smalleata they looked impressive, seen

all together that way. She felt proud of her relations, and also proud to think that if it had not been for her plan to make home with Raffles, they would not be here at all, and would probably never see TV in their lives. But then, she reflected, she would not either. It was just one of the wonderful things about having met Raffles after she had come house.

When the last of both the field mice and house mice had passed through the living room door, she and Raffles went in behind them. Only then did Uncle Stilton consider it safe to leave the sideboard. He climbed slowly down and went into the living room, taking a station just inside the door. No one could slip out without his seeing them.

31

U NCLE WENSLEYDALE, who had surrendered direction of the buffet to Uncle Stilton, had no intention of giving up an iota of his authority when it came to arranging the TV audience. For one thing Uncle Stilton had never seen a TV. He did not know a thing about it. He had probably never supervised even the smallest kind of assemblage. And now with all the house mice and the field mice gathered together, his sense of orderliness took over. He had arranged the field mice in rows on one side and the house mice in corresponding rows on the other side, with an open passage between them. It was only by being particularly quiet that Smalleata managed to find a place by Raffles on the house mouse side of the aisle.

The living room, in the faint and wavering sheen of northern lights that filtered through the windows, loomed vast and shadowy about them. Off at the far end Smalleata heard quiet movements, and as she peered into the shadows she made out the shapes of several of the flying squirrels. No one had ever seen them at a TV party before, but she was glad they had come, and if Uncle Wensleydale was aware of their presence, he did not let on. After all no one could very well object to the presence of anything as gentle as a flying squirrel.

Almost as soon as the last one had settled in his place, the brisk rapping of a stick and rapid heel taps sounded in the kitchen. They came along through the pantry and turned the corner from the hall into the living room. The moment she saw him, Smalleata knew it must be Mr. Gogie.

He was like a human person, except that he was so small. Even the top of his very tall hat, when he had it on his head, was less than two feet from the ground. It was what used to be called a top hat, and he wore an old-fashioned coat with tails, and knee breeches and stockings and shoes with buckles that sparkled faintly in the northern lights. It was hard to see much of his face, but he seemed to have a beard and cheek whiskers, without any mustache. If he was at all a human person, he was a very strange one; and then she knew that he could not be human at all for two reasons: first because she hadn't felt afraid when he came close; and second because when he spoke, she understood him perfectly, even though what he said wasn't in mouse at all. Then she saw that the flying squirrels also understood him. He was saying, politely, "I hope I'm not late."

Then it came to her that animals could understand each other and not human persons, whose language was just a series of rough and threatening sounds. But the peculiar thing about the Gogie was that even though he communicated with animals so freely, he could also do so with humans. He had visited three children of three generations of the people who lived in the house, as he once told Uncle Wensleydale, coming through the window on a moonlit night to sit on the foot of the child's bed and tell her or him stories about the brook and the farm and all the smaller beings they could not usually see but who could see *them*. Each of the three children had got his name differently — one thought it was Gogie (as it was), the second called him Mr. Woogie, and the third thought he was called Drogue. But that did not bother him. He said they could understand him, because they were young.

Now, he pulled his watch out of his breeches pocket — a tiny silver watch with a gold fob, and tilted it towards the window to read the time.

"We're just right," he announced, and pocketing the watch went over to the wall where there was a chair for small children, which he carried over to the front of the TV. When he stood on the seat, he could just reach the dials and switch. He pushed the latter and got down. Nothing happened, but that did not seem to disturb him. He backed away, watching the dark screen nonchalantly.

Suddenly the machine growled, and a series of harsh

sounds, rather like the noises old Honeysuckle, the bear, would make when he got his head in a beehive, emerged from the box. Some of the mice started to leave their seats in alarm, but the Gogie appeared to take all the commotion so plainly as a matter of course that in a moment they settled back.

Then, in the most extraordinary way, the blank screen became filled with bluish light, and out of the light a picture developed and the sound of a great many human persons. They were sitting facing a platform, just as the mice were sitting facing the picture of the platform, and from behind, if the mice also had been wearing clothes, it would have been hard to tell the difference between the screen audience and the actual mouse one. It was almost as if the mice in the living room had become members of the Congress, which was what the Gogie said they were looking at. It gave Smalleata a very strange feeling, as if she were almost like a human person, and for the first time she could think of them without dread.

Now a little group of human persons were marching down the aisle of the Congress, just as the Gogie had marched down between their seated ranks; but all the Congressmen got up on their feet, which was unsettling for the mice. They did not know whether they ought to stand up also, but as the Gogie remained seated with one leg nonchalantly crossed over the other, they stayed as they were. The little group of marching humans went briskly to the platform and the human who seemed to be the tallest of all stepped rapidly onto it, walked to the middle, where another human was standing, and turned to face the mice.

Immediately a wave of noise like water rushing into a washtub filled the TV box. It was the Congressmen clapping their hands. There was further commotion on the platform and people were shaking hands as if they were not quite sure who the other was, and then a man hit a little reading desk with a large mallet, and when silence had fallen over the confusion, he said in a resonant voice, as if he were selling liniment at a country fair, "Ladies, and GENTLEmen. The President of the United States!"

The tallest member of the group that had marched down the aisle stepped up behind the reading desk. He was a great deal taller than the man who had introduced him and had a long face and, Smalleata thought, looked sad. He put some papers on the reading desk and took a pair of glasses from his pocket and put them on. Then looking down from his height he saluted the members of the Congress and said something about "ladies and gentlemen." Then he raised his eyes so that he was looking directly from the screen and added, "And fellow Americans." It was obvious that he was addressing *them*. Smalleata glowed with pride when the Gogie translated what the President had just said, and as she looked round she saw that most of the other mice were sitting up a little straighter.

But then, as the Gogie translated, President Abraham Lyndon began to tell about the condition of the country, and she did not know whether it was so nice to be looked on as a fellow American. It appeared that the country, though it had the most resources of any nation in the world, was running short of money. There would have to be extra taxation.

Someone wanted to know what taxation meant, and Uncle Stilton said that it was like having a cheese and the Congress coming and taking all the meat out of it and leaving you the rind, which hardly seemed fair if you had been clever enough to find a whole cheese for yourself. But the President assured them that the country had never been so rich, in money, in goods, in stores of grain. Only it appeared that in some places people did not have any food at all, and it was impossible to get grain to them while there was a war going on.

Where was the war? a mouse wanted to know. And the Gogie said it was in a country way across the sea, ten thousand miles away. He said nobody knew why we were fighting there except for one or two advisers of the President, like Mr. Secretary Zwiebach. He believed that the people who lived in the northern half of the country, if they were allowed to beat the people in the southern half, would then cross over the ocean and attack America. Though to most people that did not seem very likely, as there were not as many people in the northern half of the country as there were in the single American city of New York. The trouble was that they were such a small people that the intelligent generals of the Pentagon, which was a kind of military beehive for the nation, did not know *how* to beat them. The war ought to have been over long ago, as the President explained in his sad, weary voice. He had taken all the best advice from Mr. Secretary Zwiebach on down, but the trouble was that the enemy would not admit they were beaten, even when he told them so.

"But if he took the *best* advice, the war *would* be over,

wouldn't it?" someone asked. "He must have taken the *worst* advice. Why would a President do that?"

No one knew. But suddenly a little boy mouse in the very back of the audience said, "Mother. Hasn't he got his ears on upside down?"

The President was still talking, explaining tragically that for all their stores of grain, until the war ended babies would have to go on dying of starvation in the State of Mississippi. Wherever that was.

Somehow it just did not seem to make sense to mouse minds and somewhere along the way Abraham Lyndon lost the attention of his fellow mouse Americans, though the Gogie continued to listen to every word. Uncle Wensleydale could not understand why all the masses of wheat had to be stored only where the wheat fields were. Why shouldn't there be grain elevators in the states that were usually short of food, where the poor people could get at them? This led Uncle Stilton to speculate on what it would be like to spend a winter inside of a grain elevator, and suddenly everyone felt happier, and began to think of the sumptuous buffet waiting for them on the sideboard.

The two old uncles looked meaningfully at each other, rose, and tiptoed from the room. By twos and threes the others left quietly, so as not to disturb Mr. Gogie; and in no time at all the sideboard was thronged with mice and Uncle Stilton and Uncle Wensleydale were offering tidbits to the mothers of the bride and groom and nipping the ears of the more greedy young mice who tried to push in ahead of their elders. They kept order very efficiently, and everyone agreed that the feast was delicious. They continued crowding round the two old mice until there was hardly anything left, and Uncle Wensleydale said testily, "Now, now, folks. We're keeping a snack for Mr. Gogie, if he should condescend to join us."

32

BY THIS TIME most of the mice had climbed up on the dining table and were beginning to dance. It was not like human dancing, for they all moved slowly in a circle round the table, sometimes holding hands, sometimes dancing alone and stopping suddenly to spin in one spot and then rejoining the slow procession of other dancing mice. The curious thing for Smalleata was that when she and Raffles had joined the dancers, and she let her eyes close, it was almost as if they were there alone again, like the first time he had shown her the dining room and they had climbed onto the table together. But when she opened her eyes again she could see the mice all about her, field mice and house mice, still dancing, ghostly figures in the faint glow of the northern lights.

Then the Gogie came in from the living room, in which the tired voice had stopped talking, and he hopped up on the sideboard with no effort at all. While he munched some cocktail snacks that Uncle Wensleydale, perhaps by a miracle of self-control or because he was under Uncle Stilton's stern eye, had managed to save for him,

he commented briefly that the State of the Human Union seemed going from bad to worse and they themselves should be grateful not to be involved in its woes.

Then, as he saw the mice dancing, he suddenly clicked his tongue and sprang from the sideboard to the mantelpiece where there were a couple of candlesticks with glittering glass dangles and arms for three candles — and candles in them. Pulling a match from his pocket and striking it on his pants, he climbed cleverly to the crotch of one candlestick and lighted the three candles. And a moment later he had the others lighted also, so the mice were now dancing in the soft warm glow of candlelight.

Raffles's mother, sliding by on the arm of Uncle Stilton who had come over to join in now that there was no food left in the buffet, said that they had never as long as she remembered had a dance by candlelight before. But what was most beautiful of all, Smalleata thought, was the way the candles lighted the picture of Raffles's ancestors with their wedge of cheese beside the blue ginger jar. Again it struck her how much the clever-looking mouse at the edge of the table resembled Raffles. She felt very proud to be his friend, and suddenly excited.

The Gogie came down from the mantelpiece and climbed on the table. He did not join the mouse dance but did a lively jig by himself in the middle of the table, with a rapid clatter of his tiny heels. After which he pulled a small flask from the pocket of his breeches and asked for everyone's attention. When they had all stopped dancing and turned inward to look at him, he lifted the flask and said in a high, firm voice, "I want to drink the

health of Smalleata and Raffles and their descendants forever and ever."

Then he put the flask to his lips, tipped back his head,
and emptied it at a single draft. It was, of course, a very
small flask, but then he was a very small being, yet he
went away as jauntily as he had come, his stick and
heels making a lively, diminishing tattoo through the
pantry and kitchen.

No one had ever found out how he entered the house.
No one knew where he went to when he left, but Smalleata felt a little sad because he had gone and not stayed
to see her and Raffles finish the lining of their home, especially as the time for it had now nearly come.

33

NOBODY mentioned it. It was something that she
and Raffles must decide for themselves when to do. But
she felt her heart beating faster when they left the dining table and went out into the hall.

There nearly all the young mice were playing the stair
game. They came down in twos and threes and sixes
and sevens, so fast behind each other that they were almost like a plunging river, all with their arms folded
and their tails out stiff behind them. Very few, Smalleata
observed, could do three steps at a leap the way Raffles
did. It was so exciting that when they had inched their

way upstairs they had to take a turn themselves, and she had never flown down so quickly before. As she turned with Raffles to go up once more, she saw a larger shape at the head of the stairs.

It was one of the flying squirrels. She poised and sprang. But instead of taking four or five steps as Smalleata expected, she sailed over the heads of all the racing mice, clear to the bottom of the stairs. No one had ever seen anything like it. And then another squirrel made a similar flight while all the rest looked on and applauded. No flying squirrel had ever joined in the stair game before. The fact that they had done so now would make Smalleata's and Raffles's making home always remembered.

They were back at the head of the stairs again. But this time, instead of turning to the edge of the top step to start another exciting rush down, Raffles said, "Come on, Smalleata. It's time for us to line our house."

They went into the hall that led to the bedroom he had brought her into after their first meeting in the attic; but before they reached the door he entered the bathroom and told her to stay in the middle of the floor. Then he climbed onto a chair that stood near the head of the bathtub. He jumped up onto the stretcher halfway up the back, which brought him level with the rim of the tub, and poised there.

Smalleata heard someone at her back gasp. Uncle Wensleydale had come into the bathroom. Behind him the door was suddenly filling with interested mice.

"Don't jump," Uncle Wensleydale commanded. "If you slide down into the tub there isn't any way we can get you out."

But Raffles's eyes showed his determination. He was measuring the jump he must make with the coolest care. Nothing, Smalleata realized, could stop him. She felt a chill round her heart, but at the same time it was bursting with pride. He was indeed a mouse among mice.

He jumped. His feet slithered on the slippery, enamel, rounded rim of the tub, and he scrambled wildly. But he caught his balance and in a moment started cautiously along the rim towards the foot of the tub which was close to the same wall to which the toilet tank was fastened.

Watching him, Smalleata realized that he must have made this perilous trip before to get the toilet paper with which he had decorated the caster stand, but she still could not imagine how he had done it.

By now almost all the mice had come to the bathroom door and crowded in behind Smalleata. Uncle Stilton was standing near her, looking up with the nearest expression to awe she had ever seen on his face. "Son," he was saying, "take care!"

But Raffles was obviously taking no chances he could help. His tail swung from out straight to first one side and then the other as he inched along the edge of the tub. Finally he came to where it curved towards the faucets — the nearest spot to the toilet tank.

Now he had to jump from a slippery surface. To Smalleata it looked an impossible feat. But he quickly braced his feet on the downward side of the curve and leaped, not straight for the tank, but for the wooden wall to which it was fastened. On this, in spite of its glossy paint, he got just enough hold to continue his leap onto the flat surface of the toilet tank. And there he had to pause.

"Upon my word, a carom shot!" exclaimed Uncle Stilton, who had once witnessed a game of billiards briefly from the seat of the umpire's chair, before being displaced by its rightful occupant.

Again a wave of applause swept the onlookers.

Raffles did not heed it. He was too intent on his final maneuver to feel concerned with their admiration.

Walking to the other corner of the tank top, the one nearest the roll of toilet paper on the wall opposite the bathtub, he once more gathered himself to jump. No one could understand how he managed it from such a polished surface, but he arched splendidly through the air and lit square on the large roll of toilet paper.

Immediately his weight started it turning, but this was exactly what he wanted. His tail flashed up, and he flung round to face the direction of the turn and started running with all his might. As he ran, the roll spun faster and faster. It made an impressive rolling sound. (Uncle Wensleydale declared that it reminded him of the stones in a gristmill when the sluice was full open.) And as he ran and the roll spun, the toilet paper came cascading down on the floor, till it made a small mountain far above Smalleata's head.

"Oh, Raffles!" she cried. "How wonderful! We can make the most wonderful nest in the world."

"Do you think it's enough?" he asked, still running furiously, and beginning to grow seriously breathless in the process.

"Oh, yes!" she said.

Without another word he whirled round and jumped down into the mound of the toilet paper.

No one had ever seen anything like it. In his fall he struck the descending line of paper and it broke just beneath the roller.

"Come on," he said to Smalleata, taking one corner of the broken end. She saw at once what he had in mind and snatched up the opposite corner without a word. Together they raced out of the bathroom, the long strand of toilet paper unraveling behind them. It finally got so long it broke, but before it did Uncle Stilton estimated it being almost seventy-two mouse-lengths (human persons might have called it fifteen feet).

Raffles and Smalleata never stopped. They ran down the hall with the soft white strip trailing behind them until they came to the hole near the linen cupboard which led to their own place.

"You go through," he told her, and when she was in, he began stuffing the toilet paper through to her while she pulled it from the other side. As soon as they had passed it all through the hole, he joined her and they took it to their house. They never heard one of the approving cries behind them. Perhaps some of the mice were a little envious to think of anyone's having such a luxurious home, but if they were their voices were drowned out by the rest.

In the bathroom the two old uncles stood by the remainder of the toilet paper, in case Smalleata and Raffles should return. But when they did not, they appropriated it for themselves and the two mothers, giving the latter a share largely because they needed their help in transporting such a large amount.

Meanwhile, Smalleata by herself arranged the soft white paper inside her house; a thick bedding of it on the floor and then a nest put in loosely above which she gradually shaped against the walls and ceiling. Whenever she needed more, Raffles handed it in.

Finally it was finished to her satisfaction. Nobody had ever had such a beautiful home, so soft and warm and dry. She knew it and lay down and snuggled deep in the white bed she had made and called to Raffles to come in.

Outside he said he would be there in a minute. He wanted to cork the hole that led to their home.

She lay there listening to him go away, already drowsy from all the feasting and dancing and stair game and the excitement of watching Raffles on the tub and taking home the toilet paper.

She thought sleepily of the TV which Mr. Gogie had turned on for them and the tired, sad Abraham Lyndon who was President of the Human Union, talking about his foolish war. She thought about the flying squirrels in the attic and the lady raccoon in the ceiling over the laundry. She thought about Courtenay who had volunteered to fool Reagan Ready and who had never come back. She remembered old Honeysuckle passing them in the snowy night, when Uncle Stilton had brought them house. So many beings were so much bigger, or savage, or frightening. But she was glad to be a mouse.